FIC
PAT

3-16
38749007673260G
Patterson, Raland
J. author.
 Talking Rock

Talking Rock

Raland J. Patterson

authorHOUSE

AuthorHouse™
1663 Liberty Drive, Suite 200
Bloomington, IN 47403
www.authorhouse.com
Phone: 1-800-839-8640

This book is a work of fiction. People, places, events, and situations are the product of the author's imagination. Any resemblance to actual persons, living or dead, or historical events, is purely coincidental.

© 2009 Raland J. Patterson. All rights reserved.

No part of this book may be reproduced, stored in a retrieval system, or transmitted by any means without the written permission of the author.

First published by AuthorHouse   3/17/2009

ISBN: 978-1-4389-6113-2 (e)
ISBN: 978-1-4389-6111-8 (sc)
ISBN: 978-1-4389-6112-5 (hc)

Library of Congress Control Number: 2009902489

Printed in the United States of America
Bloomington, Indiana

This book is printed on acid-free paper.

*This book is dedicated
To my wife, Ann- I love her more!
To Joe-For telling me his story.*

Table of Contents

Chapter 1.   A Chance Encounter 1
Chapter 2.   Next Date 11
Chapter 3.   Plan Completed 15
Chapter 4.   Breakfast Meeting 23
Chapter 5.   Surprise Party 27
Chapter 6.   The Party 31
Chapter 7.   Supplies 37
Chapter 8.   The Gun Show 39
Chapter 9.   An Upset Father 45
Chapter 10. A Plan Comes Together 47
Chapter 11. Second Phone Call 49
Chapter 12. Plan's First Step 51
Chapter 13. Reward For A Job Well Done 59
Chapter 14. New Revenge 61
Chapter 15. The Plan Worked 63
Chapter 16. A Senator's Wrath 67
Chapter 17. The Witness 71
Chapter 18. The Boys Are Back In Court 75
Chapter 19. A Pact 77
Chapter 20. The Next Step 81
Chapter 21. The Reporter 85
Chapter 22. Judge's Chambers 89
Chapter 23. Another Call 93
Chapter 24. Time To Kill 95
Chapter 25. A Killing 99
Chapter 26. Bill Dean Acts 103
Chapter 27. Suspect List 105
Chapter 28. Senator's Secretary 109
Chapter 29. Alibi 113
Chapter 30. New Suspect 117

Chapter 31.	Change In Plans	121
Chapter 32.	Jim's Frustration	123
Chapter 33.	Another Call	125
Chapter 34.	The Set Up	129
Chapter 35.	Dalton Sheriff	131
Chapter 36.	New Leads	135
Chapter 37.	Irene Johnson	139
Chapter 38.	Wedding Dress	143
Chapter 39.	Car Search	149
Chapter 40.	A Visit With The Senator	151
Chapter 41.	Wedding Day	157
Chapter 42.	The Honeymoon	161
Chapter 43.	Guidance	165
Chapter 44.	Finding A Truck	169
Chapter 45.	Picking Up The Truck	173
Chapter 46.	The Fbi	179
Chapter 47.	Recon The Route	183
Chapter 48.	Trial Run	185
Chapter 49.	Second Attempt	189
Chapter 50.	The Police Report	193
Chapter 51.	Finding The Killer	197
Chapter 52.	I Want A Lawyer	199
Chapter 53.	The Story	203
Chapter 54.	Hospital Room	207

Chapter 1

A Chance Encounter

In a run-down bar just outside the Atlanta city limits, a tall blond directed the bartender, "Joe, give me another beer, you wouldn't believe the horrible week I've had."

"Legs, you know my name isn't Joe. Why do you keep calling me that?"

"Felix, give me a beer, just doesn't have the same ring to it."

"You can call me Joe if you'll tell me your real name," he challenged.

"What makes you think my real name isn't Legs? Legs doesn't have a lousy job, kids and a mortgage."

He laughed. "Have it your way. Here's your beer."

Seeing a well-dressed man sitting in a back booth, she asked Joe, "Who's that guy in the back?"

"Never heard his name, but I think he's a lawyer from Cartersville. He comes in every six months or so when he needs to get drunk. He's had six vodkas so far."

"He wants to get drunk quickly. Do you think he wants some company?"

"Drunks usually do."

She observed him for a moment. He was sitting in a large, maroon leather circular booth made to seat at least eight people. She chuckled, realizing that the booth would have been a real status

1

symbol for the bar when it was in its heyday – at least twenty years ago. She couldn't understand why he chose that particular booth unless he thought it was the best; therefore, he didn't care that he was taking up so many spaces. Taking a deep breath, she walked up to him and said, "It looks like we're the only people here. Do you mind if I join you? I don't like to drink alone."

He looked up to see a striking woman with a firm, athletic body. "Please join me, but I won't make very good company. My name is Charlie."

She slid in beside him and said, "Just call me Legs. Why don't you think you would make good company?"

"My job always sucks, but today was worse than usual. I was up for senior partner of our firm, but my wonderful uncle, the Senator, promoted another guy."

Touching his hand, she asked, "Why would your uncle do that to you?"

"Oh, he says it was the best thing for our law firm. He says the new guy increased our business by 30% this year." Slurring his words, he asked, "What kind of excuse is that? I've been there ten years. I took over my father's part of the business when he died. The new guy wouldn't think I was promoted because I was his nephew, would he?"

She looked at the well-dressed drunk and mumbled, "Rich kid, weak kid."

Not understanding what she said, he asked, "What'd you say?"

"Oh nothing, just thinking out loud. What did you do before you took over your father's business?"

He looked at her like it was a stupid question and said, "I didn't do anything after law school. My family was rich. Why should I work?"

"I guess if you don't have to, it's okay. But if that's the case, why was this promotion so important to you?"

"Respect! I'm not getting the respect I deserve. One day, I'll show them. I'll show all of them. I could be just as good a Senator as my uncle. He can't live forever."

With that statement her interest was piqued. She ordered them another round and sat quietly watching while Charlie drank himself into a stupor. She studied the man before her. He had a receding hairline with curly hair. It was obvious he was vain because he refused to let his sideburns grow and, in an effort to appear younger, dyed his hair an unnatural jet black. Unfortunately, all of his efforts actually resulted in making him look as if he had a Brillo pad on the top of his head.

As she watched and listened, she began to realize that maybe her ship had finally come in. It was obvious to her Charlie was a weak, insecure man. With a little luck and a lot of planning, she just might be able to ride this horse into the winner's circle.

As she looked over at the pathetic little man, she knew he was in no shape to drive home. She'd been matching him drink for drink, so neither was she. She shook him hard and said, "We need to go home. Where do you live?"

Barely able to talk, Charlie slurred, "I'll show you. My car's out front."

"You're in no shape to drive! Your uncle would really be pissed if you got a DUI."

Hearing her say the word uncle sobered him just a little. "You're right. Let's take a taxi."

Legs yelled to the bartender, "Joe! Can you get us a taxi?"

Relieved to be getting the two drunks out of his bar, he readily agreed. "I'll have one here in a couple of minutes."

Hoping to sober Charlie up enough to get him home, she forced him to his feet and started walking him towards the door. It surprised her when she realized she was staggering too, as she never allowed herself to be out of control. The taxi was waiting when they reached the front door of the bar. She opened the car door and pushed Charlie inside. Then she staggered around to the other side. She heard the driver ask, "Where to, lady?"

"I'm not sure." Shaking Charlie, she said, "Charlie, he needs to know where you live."

Trying to sound in control, Charlie handed a business card to the driver and said, "Cartersville."

The driver said, "It's not worth my while to go all the way to Cartersville."

Charlie handed him a hundred dollar bill without flinching. It was obvious he had done this before. The money disappeared into the driver's hand as he said, "Sit back, relax and I'll have you home before you know it."

Legs soon dozed off from the heat in the cab. When the driver hit a loose manhole cover the noise awakened her. She could see they were in an old, established residential section of town. Majestic oaks framed both sides of the road creating an umbrella effect over the street. *So this is where the rich folks live in Cartersville,* she thought. As they continued slowly down the street, she noticed some of the residences had signs out front. One was a law firm, one an architect, and one was even a museum. It looked as if over the years these magnificent homes had been bought and renovated into prestigious businesses. The driver slowed and turned into a driveway saying, "Here you are, ma'am. Do you need help getting him inside?"

"I would really appreciate that." They got him to the front door, Charlie was able to hand her his key. She opened the door and heard the shrill sound of an alarm system. Panicked, she turned to Charlie and said, "What's the alarm code?"

His words were so slurred they could barely make out that the alarm wasn't turned on before he passed out. With the driver's help, she got him to the first bedroom they could find. Once the driver had left, she searched the house for a room of her own. Two doors down, she met with success. Kicking off her shoes, she fell onto the bed and was asleep before her head hit the pillow.

The sound of the morning newspaper hitting the front door awakened her. It took her a moment to remember where she was and the events of the previous evening. Barely able to sit up, she began to glance around the room. It was elegant and understated, just like she had always imagined the rich lived. She walked over to the window and thought, *My God, this is an estate. The yard is half a block long and just as wide.*

Looking closer, she noticed that the grass and shrubbery had been meticulously manicured. She again faced the room and slowly took in the details. It was then she realized what had been bothering her. There was no way Charlie could take care of this huge place by himself. She entered the bathroom and cleaned up before walking downstairs. Charlie was sitting at the dining room table.

Her presence startled him. "Who the hell are you and what are you doing in my house?"

The tone of his voice pissed her off. Her normal response to his rudeness would have been to tell him to screw himself; however, the beginning of a plan was forming in her mind to use this weak, useless creature. Biting her tongue, she said, "I'm Legs. Don't you remember last night?"

Still slightly drunk, he said, "I thought that was a weird dream."

"Are you disappointed?"

Remembering his manners, he stood quickly and said, "No way. Can I have Juanita make you some breakfast?"

"That would be great. You have a beautiful home and yard."

"I ought to, with two gardeners, a maid and a cook to do the work."

Seeing his business card lying on the table, she picked it up and read it. *Charles D. Webb, Attorney-at-Law.*

"Charles Webb, with your life you should never be depressed about anything, but I'm glad you were last night."

"I'm glad, too."

When Juanita brought in her breakfast, Legs inhaled the wonderful smell and it almost took her breath away. "God, that smells good."

Juanita smiled at the compliment and said, "Thank you, ma'am."

Legs buttered her toast and said, "Thank you! It's been a long time since I was served breakfast."

Charlie was pleased with her response. He glanced down and realized he only had on his boxer shorts under his bathrobe. He stood and said, "If you don't mind, I'll go get dressed while you're eating."

She could see he was uncomfortable, so she smiled and said, "No problem. I'll be right here until the food runs out." As she watched him leave she smiled and thought, *Oh, my God, I've hit the jackpot. This guy is perfect! All it will take is me stroking his ego and keeping him happy. He's rich and weak, but he has the potential to actually become a Senator with my help. He can probably count the number of times he's gotten any on one hand. With me, he's going to think he has died and gone to heaven. I'm going to give him more sex than he has ever dreamed about. I only need a simple plan for a weak, simple man.*

Sipping her coffee, she thought back to when she was called Legs for the first time. While in high school she couldn't say she was homely; it was more like she was invisible. No one, especially the boys, knew she was alive. Then one summer her mother got her a job cleaning offices for some of the businessmen in town. An older man, about 40, looked at her like no one else ever had. It scared and excited her at the same time. When she picked up his trash he gave out a little whistle and asked, "Hey there, Legs, where did you come from?"

She had giggled and raced away. However, his flirting was exciting and she liked it.

Talking Rock

From then on, she made a special effort to make sure he was at his desk when she cleaned his office. She knew it was a dangerous game, but this older man made her feel special.

Then one day he asked, "So Legs, how old are you?"

She thought, *Should I lie? Why, he probably already knows.*

She answered, "I just turned 17."

"Jailbait, that's what I thought."

She didn't know what to say. Standing there like a scared rabbit, she couldn't move.

He broke the awkward silence by saying, "That means I can't touch but I can still look, if that's okay with you."

That short phrase—'if that's okay with you'-- changed her life forever. Someone thought she was important enough to ask her opinion and permission. All summer long the flirting increased between them. After a couple of months on the new job she was given sole responsibility for his section of the office. It didn't go unnoticed with him that she always cleaned his office last.

One day he asked, "Are you working this Friday?"

Surprised, she replied, "Yes, why?"

"Well the office staff is going on a picnic at noon and taking the rest of the day off. It'll be just you and me kid," he said, laughing.

The thought of just the two of them alone together excited her. When Friday came she didn't wear her usual work clothes but chose a thin cotton dress that hit her long legs at about mid thigh. When she walked into his office that Friday afternoon she was weak in the knees. The expression on his face was more than she expected. He gave out his normal whistle and said, "My God. Your legs do go all the way to heaven."

His comment washed over her like nothing she had ever felt before. Then he said something that had a profound effect on her future. "I'll give you $100 to see where those legs stop."

When she heard that, she wasn't upset or offended. She just heard $100. That was a week's salary. Before she thought, she blurted out, "A real $100?"

Not letting the opportunity drop he answered, "Yes. I promise to only look."

"You just look and nothing else for $100?"

Opening his wallet he placed two fifty-dollar bills on the top of his desk. Grabbing the money she stepped back and raised her dress above her waist. He just stared at the beautiful, young body in front of him. After what seemed like enough time, she dropped her dress. He liked what he saw. He then asked, "How much would it cost me for you to take your panties off?"

She surprised herself when she snapped back, "A lot more. Let's just stay with the $100 look for a while."

As time passed he saw more; however, he paid more also. The attention he gave her began to improve her self-esteem. She was making about a thousand dollars a month just selling him looks. His constant compliments on her legs created the desire to make them even better. She began a workout routine that created a perfect, athletic body. Smiling at the thought, even the high school boys began to notice her. She'd been flattered when the richest boy in town asked her to the prom. However, when her dream date turned out to be a put-out-or-get-out affair, something snapped in her. She got out of the car and began to walk out of the woods where they had parked. The more she walked the angrier she got. She had walked only 500 yards when her date pulled up beside her. Thinking he was still in control, he called out, "Get in this car."

She yelled back, "Only if you'll take me to the police station."

She hadn't known it at the time, but the rich kid was in constant trouble with the police. He folded like a house of cards. The self-assured, rich kid disappeared before her eyes and a whining, scared child replaced him. Begging her forgiveness, he promised her anything she wanted not to tell on him. His response was instrumental in Legs' development of the philosophy she began to live by: *Show me a rich kid and I'll show you a wimp that can be fleeced.*

Over the years her relationship with the old man became more and more intimate. He seemed to get the most pleasure from giving pleasure. He taught her the pleasure of oral sex on his large, walnut desk. The price for this was her college education. His strange sense of honor about not taking her virginity allowed her to remain a virgin until her freshman year of college. She regretted telling him about her affair with a classmate, as he seemed to lose the gleam in his eye when he looked at her after that. But her approach on life was set. Find the weak, rich kids and take them for all they were worth. She prided herself on how quickly she could recognize them. Since then, she had developed an alter-ego--Legs-- as a coping mechanism for dealing with the fact that these very men had used her then tossed her aside at will. As Legs, she became the hunter seeking gratification and dreams she could never achieve in her ordinary life. The previous week had been extremely stressful and she smiled as she realized it was time for Legs to come out and play.

Chapter 2

Next Date

When Charlie came back downstairs, they just sat at the table and talked until almost noon. Finally, Charlie called them a cab and they rode back to the bar to get their cars. Legs was frustrated that Charlie hadn't said anything about seeing her again. She began to worry that a sober Charlie was too timid and shy to make her plan work.

When he paid the driver she took the bull by the horns. "Charlie Webb, I had an awesome time. When can we do this again?"

He was speechless. *This beautiful woman wanted to see him again?*

Impatiently she said, "I have to work all next week, but I'm free Saturday. How about you?"

With a big grin, he said, "I'm free all weekend. When can I pick you up?"

Legs didn't want him to know where she lived, so she quickly said, "Why don't I just come to your house and we'll go from there?"

He was so excited, he'd agree to anything. It was clear that he might have seen his 40th birthday, but if her plan was going to work, she would have to treat him like a naïve sixteen year old. She decided that the less information she gave him about herself the better. He needed to think he was the center of her world if she was going to convince him he was capable of the things she wanted him to achieve. Pumping up his ego was really important; because it was obvious no one had ever told Charlie they thought he could do anything. While time consuming, it would be worth it. Of all her past efforts, this one seemed to have the most potential.

Legs invested hundreds of hours over a period of six months gaining Charlie's trust. Her gut told her Charlie now viewed his uncle as the only obstacle between him and a senate seat. She knew the key to success was for Charlie to believe killing his uncle was his idea and that her only role was to assist him in achieving this goal. "Charlie if your uncle were dead, would you get the senate seat?"

His grin showed he approved of the idea, "I would be the obvious choice. I'm the last Webb."

Anyone observing the mismatched pair would think they were mother and son, not lovers. Legs was at least four inches taller than Charlie and with her toned and athletic body she was quite striking. Seeing her smile with pleasure when he called her Legs, Charlie realized it wasn't important that she hadn't told him her real name. On the other hand, with his weak chin and mousy appearance, he had been nicknamed 'weasel' during his high school years. Using her sexual powers she had slowly taken control of the insecure drunk she had found months before.

With a matter of fact tone she said, "You need to find a Springfield 03 rifle."

"Why a 03?"

"That was the weapon of choice of a serial killer here in Georgia." She laughed and continued, "I'm sure he won't mind getting the credit for taking out a few more."

"I'm not sure where to find one."

Having anticipated the question, Legs said, "There's a gun shop on the north side of Atlanta called Kurt's Place."

"I know the one you're talking about. It's over next to Doraville? I've driven by it a hundred times."

"That's the place. It's big enough that they won't remember who bought the rifle. Make sure you pay cash so they can't trace it."

"I'll go by and pick it up this afternoon after work."

Later that night, Legs phoned Charlie to check on his progress. He answered on the first ring.

"Did you get the job done?"

"Yeah, I was in and out in less than 20 minutes."

"Do you think the clerk will remember you buying it?"

"I don't think so. He had four others like it on the shelf. When I was paying for it another guy bought two."

"Where is it now?"

"I've got it in the trunk of my car. I thought I would go practice some with it tomorrow. If we're really going to do this thing I need to be ready."

"You can shoot, can't you?"

"Oh yeah, next time you visit I'll show you my marksmanship badges."

Frustrated, but determined not to show it, she said, "I forgot you were a poor little rich kid. But if we are going to make this plan work you need to be a man, not a boy."

Her remarks hurt but he kept his feelings to himself. Trying to get her attention away from him he asked, "Who's first?"

"Let's not talk about that over the phone."

The next evening they were both eager to discuss the plan. Sounding like a kid on Christmas morning, Charlie bragged to Legs about his shooting ability. Patiently, she listened and then casually steered the conversation towards the plan and who their first target should be. "I was thinking Ben Gibson and his son would be perfect, they fit the pattern of an old serial killer here in Georgia to the tee."

"What kind of pattern?'

"The killer targeted fathers and sons that used their money and power to run roughshod over the people in their towns. They always felt they were so special and that the law and everyone else were there just to serve them. In fact, in most cases they felt they were above the law. The killer always went to great efforts to make it look like a murder/suicide and the fact that you've never heard about it proves he was very successful. No one really knows how many people he killed before he stopped."

"How do you know all that?"

Lying, she said, "I used to date a guy with the Georgia Bureau of Investigations and he was always bragging about a big case his boss couldn't solve."

"You dated a GBI agent?"

"When I was a young and naïve, a couple of cops, too. You don't want to know what I learned from that experience."

"Why did you pick the Gibsons?"

"Well, old Ben has the money and it won't be the first time he bailed Ray out of trouble."

"How do you know about them?"

"From college, Ray and some of his high school buddies raped one of the girls in the dorm. Old-man Gibson gave her $50,000 to keep her mouth shut."

Wide-eyed, he asked, "Did she take it?"

"Sure she did. From what I heard she and Ray made the whole thing up in the first place. The rumor was they split the money." She didn't feel it was necessary to let Charlie know she was the co-ed.

He smiled and said, "Then this should be easy."

She snapped back, "Don't underestimate Ben Gibson. He started one of the first carpet mills in Dalton, which is still the largest in the county. He's a member of every club and is president of a lot of them."

Cowering in his chair, he answered, "If he's so well liked maybe we should do someone else."

"He's the right guy. With all that going for him, he still has a major weak spot – his son."

A big smile came over his face as he said, "When do we start?"

"You just keep practicing. I need to get some other information first. I think we should be ready to call old Ben in about a week or so."

Chapter 3

Plan Completed

Legs asked, "How did practice go?"

Smiling, he said, "I can hit a Coke bottle at 150 yards even in a strong wind."

"Don't get cocky. We're talking serious business here," she snapped back.

His insecurity came rushing back, he timidly asked, "What did you find out?"

"Just as I thought, Ray is still a low life. If anything, he's gotten worse. The mere mention of his name prompts people to start telling their own horror stories."

"So, it's still a go on Gibson?"

"Oh yeah, it's fate. I thought it would be hard to get his private phone number, but would you believe it was in the phone book?"

"Are you sure? It was that easy?"

"Yeah, I called the number and he answered."

"Does that mean we're ready?"

"Yes, I guess so." Looking him straight in the eyes she said, "Charlie, are you sure about this? You know once we start, there's no turning back."

Returning her stare, he said with confidence, "I have never been more certain about anything in my whole life. It's time people knew what a great man I am."

Leaning back in her chair, she asked, "How busy is your schedule for the next couple of months?"

"Not busy at all. Most of my clients are getting old. I have most of their estate planning done. I just collect their money. The only problem I see is if one of them should die; otherwise, I'm here to service my beauty queen."

Moving closer she said, "You really hate being a lawyer, don't you?"

"Yeah. That was my father's thing." His face got red as he continued, "Everybody thought he was so perfect."

"He did leave you his practice when he died."

Still flushed, he said, "You know how bad it is to live in your old man's shadow? I want people to respect me. I'm still referred to as his son, as if that's the only thing I have going for me. It's been ten years since his death. I'm tired of it."

Legs had been working Charlie's ego for more than six months. She felt it was time to initiate their plan to make him a Senator; and better still, to make her a Senator's wife. Making up her mind quickly, she said, "Good! Then we'll make the first call tonight. Before you call, tell me again what you're going to say."

"I'll call Gibson and tell him I'm the father of a teenage girl that Ray got pregnant. I'll demand he give us $250,000 or I'll kill his son."

"I hope you are more convincing than that or he'll just laugh at you."

Sounding like a little kid he said, "He better not."

He could hear her disappointment in her voice as she said, "I think I better write you a script if this is going to work."

He snapped back, "I can do it. I don't need a script."

"What are you going to tell him to write in his note?"

She had rendered him speechless for a moment, "I forgot about the note."

"Never mind, go to church and I'll write out exactly what you need to say."

Charlie yelled, "Church? Are you kidding me?"

Taking his hand, she explained in a calm voice, "No, if we're going to do this, we have to go all the way. It's really important now that you improve your relationships with Georgia's elite. Southern gentlemen never miss a Sunday church service. You need to keep rubbing elbows with the in-crowd. If you're going to be a Senator you need to start now."

Smiling, Charlie answered, "You think of everything, don't you?"

Patting his hand with a smile, she answered, "Let's hope so. I'm too young and beautiful for prison."

While her partner attended church, she wrote a detailed script, which left nothing to chance. She even included a variety of answers for different responses. When he returned she had him read it aloud until she was satisfied he was convincing.

Finally she handed him the phone. "That last time was perfect. Let's make the call before you forget. Remember, pretend you're talking to your father and make him listen."

That analogy hit a nerve with him and he stated emphatically, "I will. I've always wanted to give him a piece of my mind."

As she dialed the phone for Charlie she directed him, "The phone is ringing. Put the washcloth over the mouthpiece."

Gibson answered, "Ben Gibson here."

"Gibson, you're the bastard I wanted to talk to. Your son got my 17-year-old pregnant and I want to know what you're going to do about it."

In a calm voice, Gibson answered, "Sir, I think you have the wrong number."

In a lower, but strong voice, Charlie asked, "Do you have a son named Ray?"

"Yes, I do."

"Well then, I've got the right number. Your son came to Ringgold pretending to be a college student. He got Judy pregnant. What are you going to do about it?"

Uncomfortable, and trying to get off the phone, he answered, "I'm not sure there is anything I can do."

"Well, if you can't, I can. I'll kill the little bastard. That was my first reaction, but I knew that wouldn't help Judy. I thought I'd give you a chance to make it right. Her life is ruined."

Still trying to deflect the subject, Gibson explained, "I understand what you're feeling, but what do you want me to do? My son is a grown man. I can't control him."

"I want that devil's seed in my daughter's belly cut out. I want you to pay for it."

Seeing a way to make the caller go away, Gibson replied, "I can do that, I know a doctor that can do it."

"I figured you'd know someone. From what I hear it's not your first grandchild. But that's not all…"

Gibson asked, "What else?"

"Afterwards, I want to move my daughter someplace far away from here – someplace like Florida or California, so she can start her life over. We'll need money for that."

"How much money are we talking about?"

Charlie answered, "$200,000."

Stammering, Gibson said, "$200,000? I can't pay that."

"Now it's $250,000. Every time you say no, the number goes up. I don't think you know how serious I am. After the third no, I'll just kill the bastard. Do I make myself clear?"

Trying to regain control of the situation, in his best and strongest voice, Gibson said, "Sir, you know I'll need proof before I put out that kind of money."

"You want proof? I'll tell you what. Why don't you and Ray meet me and my daughter at the Sheriff's office tomorrow morning at 8 a.m.? I like that better. He goes to jail and we can sue you for everything you're worth. I'll bet everybody in your county knows Ray. I'll see you tomorrow morning. Goodbye."

"**Wait. Wait.** Let's talk," he begged.

"Why should I? I'm tired of you rich people always getting your way."

"Don't hang up. I know we can work something out. How far along is she?"

"Nearly two months. What's that got to do with it?" Charlie asked.

"So she's not showing yet?"

"Not yet."

"Well, I think we can make this go away and get you moved."

"Now you're talking." Reading down the list Legs had given him, Charlie said, "I have one last requirement."

Almost in a whisper, Gibson asked, "What's that?"

"You seem to be a man of your word."

In a stronger voice, he answered, "I am."

"I want you to write out a note in your own handwriting stating that your son will never do this again. I want my daughter to know she's done the right thing by not sending him to jail."

"What do you want me to say?"

"Do you have something to write with?"

"Yes sir, I'm ready."

"Start with, 'I'm so sorry my son has abused young women. I'll make sure he will never do it again. God forgive him and me.' Then sign it. Put the note in the bag of money. I'll give it to my daughter. Make sure she never has to show it to a jury in the future."

"I've done it. I'll make sure Ray behaves himself."

"How long will it take to contact the doctor and get the money?"

"I'll talk to him tomorrow, but it'll take a couple of weeks to get that much money together."

"Good. Let's do everything at one time. I'll call you in about 10 days."

He hung up.

Legs was pleased with how well Charlie had handled the phone call. She pulled him into her arms and whispered, "I love it when you take charge. You've got me so hot, let's do it right here on the table."

After Charlie's reward was over Legs was all business. While putting her clothes back on she began to give him instructions. "Charlie, for the next couple of weeks you need to watch Gibson's house."

Sheepishly he asked, "What am I looking for?"

"We need the family routine if we're going to make our plan work. Do you have a good pair of binoculars?"

Pulling his pants up, he said, "I think I have some in the trunk of my car."

Turning towards the door, she directed, "Let's go see."

They both walked outside and Charlie opened his trunk.

Seeing the cluttered trunk she barked, "My God. What happened to your trunk? It looks like a trash dump. Look here. You've got shells rolling around everywhere. Are these the bullets you're going to use on the Gibsons?"

"Yeah, they look okay to me."

"Where's the box they came in?"

"It's in there someplace. Just move that stuff out of the way. Let me help."

Slapping his hand, she snapped, "No. Get out of my way. I'll do it."

She picked up the ammo box and began to put the 30-06 shells back inside. Closing the flap she directed, "Now only take one out at a time as you need them. This is enough ammunition to kill ten people. With any luck we'll never need to buy anymore. So take care of it. Did you find those binoculars?"

"I think they're behind the spare tire," he said, pointing.

Picking them up she snarled, "Those things are too small. They look like opera glasses."

"That's what they are. What's the problem?"

Shaking her head, "I'll never understand your lifestyle. You rich people live in a world of your own."

"I thought you liked my world. Isn't that why we are doing this? So I can stay in this pampered world and you can join me?"

Smiling, "Oh, Charlie. You're right. It's just that I get frustrated at times. I want everything to be perfect and let's face it. You're the most disorganized person I know."

Smiling back at her, "Isn't that one of the reasons you fell in love with me?"

Nodding her head, "You're right." She hoped he never learned that she was not in the relationship because of her love for him but because of her love of power.

"Did we just have a fight?"

Looking up at him from beneath the trunk lid, "I guess we did. Why?"

Smiling, "Doesn't that mean make-up sex?"

"Oh, Charlie. What am I going to do with you?"

"Make love to me, I hope."

"Okay, I need to relax too, but when we finish we need to get a strong spotting scope."

"I promise, I promise."

She loved the sexual power she had over him.

Chapter 4

Breakfast Meeting

In conversation with Private Investigator Sam Wright, Jim Coleman said, "Let's have breakfast at the Fountain in the morning."

"Sounds good to me. What's up?"

"I need to close some loose ends without being interrupted." answered Jim.

"What time?"

"Eight o'clock should be good. The breakfast crowd will be gone by then."

Jim arrived a little early to relax over his first cup of coffee. At a quarter to eight Sam came through the door. Jim waved him over to his table, saying, "Don't tell me it's that Army thing again."

Smiling and standing a little taller, Sam repeated an old saying "If an Army officer arrives on time he's fifteen minutes late."

"Would you explain one thing to me? You were a state patrol officer four times longer than you were an army officer. I've never met a cop who shows up anywhere on time. What's different about you?"

"As an officer I got used to working with people I could trust and it made me feel special to know they could always depend on me. Being on time is one way of showing people I will be there when they need me."

"Mr. GI Joe, I can't believe you made fun of me and my westerns. Does Jane know you're a modern-day Sir Galahad?"

"Listen to who's talking, Mr. Don Quixote. Which windmills are we tilting today?"

Waving to the waitress, Jim said, "Let's get some eggs with gravy and biscuits before we go to work." They made quick work of the southern breakfast.

"Sam, I'm returning Senator Webb's retainer and closing the case. He seemed pissed when I called him. Is there something I don't know that I should?"

"Not really. Like I said, his son is guilty as hell. He should go to jail until he grows up, but we know that's not going to happen as long as the Senator pulls strings for him."

"I agree, but the chances of his son growing up are slim at best. Speaking of growing up, how are Sue McGill's son and that Crawford boy doing?

A big smile came over Sam's face. "Johnny and Doug are doing great. All they needed was a little male guidance in their lives."

"I saw some of that guidance when you helped them pick up trash all the way from West Fannin to Blue Ridge."

Sam blushed in spite of himself, saying, "I think Jane and the kids enjoyed it as much as I did."

"Damn, I didn't know you made a family project of it. I now know I hired the right man. I bet if you hadn't killed Green when he shot you, you'd be thanking him for ending your Georgia State Patrol career."

With a sheepish grin, Sam whispered, "I hate to admit it, but I'm grateful for the career change, but I sure could do without the arthritis in my shoulder."

"You know, before you came in I was drinking coffee and thinking about how fate has changed both of our lives. I came here with vengeance in my heart but luck led me to Mike and Mother Barkley."

Sam added, "Don't forget Peggy. If you hadn't met her, you wouldn't have JM. In fact you wouldn't even have become a lawyer."

"You're right. I still can't get past Peggy being executed for her brother and father's death."

"If you think about it, something wonderful came from two awful events. Peggy's death in your case and Green's in mine."

"That's true. In the last year do you realize how busy you've been? You've killed the man that shot your partner, become a fingerprint expert, found evidence to clear four of our clients and taken two delinquent boys under your wing and mentored them. I don't care who you are – that's an awesome thing."

Smiling, Sam asked, "Is it too soon to ask for a raise?"

Chapter 5

Surprise Party

Looking at her calendar, Dr. Amanda Hicks was surprised to see that she had an open afternoon. Going out to her receptionist's desk, she asked, "Is my calendar correct? I don't have any appointments this afternoon?"

"That's right, Dr. Mandy. You had two cancellations that rescheduled for next week."

"That's wonderful. I've got something important to do. I'm leaving now and will see you tomorrow."

Nancy looked up from her desk and said, "Dr. Mandy, this is the first time you have ever taken time off. I hope nothing is wrong."

"Nothing's wrong. I just need to do something I've wanted to do for months."

As Amanda walked to the parking lot she felt almost giddy. She hadn't felt this way since she was a little girl in Richmond. She decided to go to the Barkley's first. Mike and Mother Barkley were the keys to her plan. They had retired from the post office just six months before. Thinking about how they had taken Jim under their wings a decade ago gave her a warm feeling all over. They had become like parents to Jim and her, and Jim's son JM considered them his grandparents. She knew this because Mike had been the postmaster for over forty years and there was no one in the county who didn't know and like the big man. He was known for his jokes, but most of all, for his big, infectious belly laugh.

It made her feel a little sad when she thought about how the Barkleys had lost their son, Michael, in Vietnam and how quickly they were ready to accept Jim in their lives six years after Michael's death. Because Jim had brought Mother and Mike out of their mourning, he was liked by anyone who called them friends. The first sign that the Barkleys were on their way to recovery was when people began to hear Mike's laugh around the post office. She remembered her first few meetings with Jim could be described as bumpy at best. Being the strong, independent personality that she was, she tried to take charge of the relationship with Jim when she realized he was infatuated with her. She couldn't help but smile when she remembered how he had lost his temper and had thrown her in the lake, saying the chilling words to her, "I'm not your daddy, so I don't have to like you." That had been almost four years ago. Now she knew she could never love another man like she loved him.

When she drove into the Barkley's driveway, they ran out to meet her. Mother was the first to speak. "Mandy! Is there something wrong? Is it Jim?"

She could see the fear in Mother's face and soothed her by saying, "Nothing is wrong. In fact, it's just the opposite. I was thinking about planning a surprise birthday party for Jim."

With a big laugh, Mike said, "To be such a little thing, you sure can come up with some big ideas. Girl, I like it."

Amanda hugged the big man saying, "I'm so glad. Do you think we can keep it from him?"

"That'll be the easy part. He's so involved with his work he wouldn't notice if the north side of Blue Ridge fell into the Toccoa River. Little girl, where do you plan to have this shindig?"

"I was thinking the Circle J Steak House would be nice."

"That new restaurant next to Lance's trucking?"

"That's the one. I checked it out. There's a big room in the back where the Kiwanis Club meets on Mondays."

Mother asked, "When do you plan on having the party?"

"His birthday is the last Sunday of the month, so I was thinking the Saturday before."

Together, Mother and Mike said, "Perfect."

Mother asked, "How will you get him there without giving away the surprise?"

"Let me worry about that," answered Mandy.

Chapter 6

The Party

Mike was pleased to see how many of their friends were showing up for Jim's birthday. Sam and Jane exchanged hugs with Mike and Mother as they arrived.

"Mike, I think everybody in the county is here," said Sam.

"All I said was the food would be free," said Mike, letting out one of his big laughs.

A man with the manners of a southern gentleman approached him saying, "Easy with that laugh, Mike. These are new windows."

"I'll be doggone," said Mike. "Sam I want you to meet Joe Chancey. Some say he can make water run uphill."

Shaking his hand, Sam said, "I don't think I've ever met anyone with such a powerful reputation."

Joe smiled, and said, "You know how Mike likes to embellish the truth."

Defending himself, Mike said, "Sam, you may be interested in what Joe did back in the thirties."

Looking at Sam, Joe asked, "He's not a revenuer, is he?"

"No, but he was a state patrolman. He's Jim's private investigator now," answered Mike.

"Are you the patrolman that got shot by old man Green's boy?" asked Joe.

"I'm afraid that was me."

"Good shooting. I heard you put three in his chest after he shot you."

Red-faced, he answered, "I was just doing my job the best I could." Then, changing the subject, he asked, "What was it you did back in the thirties?"

Joe took the bait. "We used to make a little moonshine."

Mike insisted, "Joe, tell him how you made it."

That's all the encouragement it took for Joe to start in. "I'd pay four dollars for 100 pounds of sugar, a dollar for a bushel of cornmeal and a dollar for a bushel of barley malt. That would make thirty gallons of corn liquor. We sold it for ninety cents a gallon."

Doing some figuring on his hands, Sam said, "That's twenty-three dollars profit. How much was that back then? That must have been a week's pay."

"Oh Lord. Twenty-three dollars was a lot of money. Most working people were only making a dollar a day."

"How many people did you have to split that with?"

"Just one, my brother Chesley. Everybody called him Bear because he was hairy all over. He used to drink a lot; about the second day we worked the still he'd get drunk. At first we made brandy. What's bad about brandy is you can get drunk on it one day, go to sleep, get up the next morning, drink a glass of water and you'd be drunk again. Bear made a habit of it."

"How long did it take you to work off a batch?"

"About five days."

"Was it hard to find buyers?"

"Nah, we had a friend that lived up at Higdon's store. You know that's up next to Hell's Holler. He said he'd take all we could make. When we'd run off a batch we'd let him know and he'd send someone to get it."

"How often would you make a run?"

"Let's say we kept him well stocked."

Then getting serious he continued, "You know, I liked to make moonshine. I really did."

Mike chimed in and said, "You sound like Mother when she's making her preserves."

Smiling, Sam said, "I guess the revenuers put you out of business."

"Not really. The price of sugar got so high, we couldn't make a profit."

They all laughed, but as usual, Mike was the loudest. Mother ran over and grabbed Mike's arm saying, "Would you be quiet? Mandy and Jim are in the parking lot."

Outside, Jim opened Amanda's door saying, "This is a great idea! I haven't had a steak in six months."

Teasing him, Amanda said, "Wait until I tell Mother you're tired of her cooking."

Apologetic, he said, "You know what I mean. Steak, potato and a beautiful woman - it doesn't get any better than that."

As they entered the restaurant, Jim asked the hostess, "How does this work?"

"Sir, you and your wife just follow the line. Take a tray and you'll see the menu items on the wall. Jenny will take your order and give you a number. You pay at the register and then take the number to any table you want. They'll bring your food as soon as it's ready."

"Thank you, ma'am, but Mandy isn't my wife yet." Looking at Mandy, he said, "That didn't sound very good, did it?"

As Jim and Mandy moved forward, Jenny approached them and said, "Sir, you're our one hundredth customer and win a free meal. Would you mind following me to the office for a picture and your certificate?"

Jim took Mandy's hand in his and said, "Sure thing. Just lead the way."

As they came around the corner, the trio was met with a loud "Surprise!" and a chorus of Happy Birthday. Jim was speechless; all this was just for him. He didn't want to say it but he'd never had a birthday party before. He could see Mike's head above the crowd and could hear his booming voice drowning out the others. He turned to

Mandy and said, "This feels like something you might have come up with."

She laughed and squeezed his hand saying, "With a lot of help from Mother and Mike. We love you. Happy Birthday."

He looked around and realized he only knew about half of the people there. Sam and Jane came over and pulled Mandy and him to the center of the room where a three-tier cake sat with three large candles – one for each decade. As Jim started to blow them out, someone yelled "Make a wish first!"

He smiled and said, "I already have." Then he blew out the candles. After cutting the cake everyone stood around in small groups joking and laughing. Jim still couldn't believe that so many people had come to his surprise party. He felt a warm feeling come over him that he'd never really experienced before. Smiling to himself he realized that it had been a while since someone had said to him 'You're not from here, are you?'

Nick and Betty Turner came over to wish him a Happy Birthday. Jim couldn't believe the change in Old Nick since he had married Betty. It was apparent that he had given up drinking. Joking with Jim, Nick said, "The kid that came into the Supper Club bar more than a decade ago is now a man."

Jim agreed with his comment saying, "I guess I was a kid then, but I remember I didn't like you telling me so."

Patting Jim on the back, Nick said, "That's what friends are for. They tell it like it is."

Jim smiled and said, "I guess it's my turn then."

Nick asked, "What's on your mind?"

"Ah, just that marrying Betty was the best thing you ever did."

Betty grabbed Jim and gave him a big hug, saying, "Jim, that's the nicest thing I've ever heard. Thank you."

Red-faced, Jim tried to change the subject. "Nick, what's new?"

Laughing at Jim's embarrassment, Nick took the bait. "Have you heard that since the sheriff fired old Deputy Cagle, he got himself a job in Jasper as a PI?"

"No, I hadn't. At least he's not a cop anymore."

"I agree. There's nothing worse than a crooked cop."

As they were talking Sue McGill walked up and gave Jim a big hug, "Happy Birthday. I have a special gift from Johnny." She handed him a small box.

When he opened it, he smiled and lifted the item from the box. "Just what I needed. A new top water plug." He looked a Mandy and said, "I guess we need to go fishing tomorrow."

Taking the plug from him, she said, "Do I need to wear a bathing suit?"

"I don't know. If you want to you can. Why?"

Smiling and trying to look coy she said, "I was just wondering if you were planning to throw me in the lake again."

Everyone laughed as Jim blushed, "Aren't you ever going to forget that?"

Making sure she spoke loudly enough for everyone to hear she said, "Are you kidding? I know when I've found a good horse to ride."

Sue asked, "Jim when are you going to make an honest woman out of her? I remember a couple of months ago in Ellijay when you were running for judge, you made a wonderful speech about commitment. Was that just political rhetoric?"

He turned to Mandy and placed a hand on each of her shoulders. "How about Thanksgiving Day, Miss Hicks?"

It took a few minutes for her to realize what he was saying and she screamed, "Mother Barkley! Can you handle a wedding on that day?"

"Lordy, Lordy, child. You know I can. I'll just add a wedding cake to the menu."

Everyone crowded around the couple and congratulated them.

Chapter 7

Supplies

Looking through Charlie's closet Legs asked, "Do you have an old, worn pair of jeans – the older the better?"

"I don't think I've ever worn jeans," he answered.

Turning quickly, Legs said, "Are you kidding me?"

"No. Mother said only trailer-trash wear blue jeans."

"Well, it's time you found out jeans are in fashion now."

"Why do you want me to wear jeans anyway? I'm too old to follow fashion."

"Because there's a gun show in Atlanta this weekend and we're going."

"Now why in the world would I do that?" he asked.

"Because if we are going to get you a Senator's seat we'll need two more Springfield rifles. What better place to buy them than a gun show where we'd leave no trail?"

Clearly turned on he pulled her into his arms. "Honey, it always surprises me how well you plan things."

"It's only that you've never had to work for anything. You don't realize how many little things it takes to complete a plan well," she answered.

"You know, meeting you was the best thing that ever happened to me."

She smiled, "Don't you ever forget it. However, we were destined to meet because we both want and need the same things – riches and power. If you stay with me, we'll have them both."

Charlie tried to pull her into his arms and whispered, "You turn me on when you talk like that."

Pushing him away, "I think you stay turned on."

Stepping back a few feet, "Is that bad? I'm only that way when I'm around you. You make me hot. What gets you hot?"

Thinking for a minute, "When I achieve a major goal I get so excited I could screw on Main Street."

Moving near her again, "I can't wait to see that."

She pushed him away and in her purely business tone of voice, said, "Keep listening to me and you'll see it. Right now we need to attend that gun show this coming weekend."

In an effort to get back on her good side, he said, "I'm ready."

"Not really, but you will be. Let's go to the Goodwill store and get you some redneck clothes and boots."

In disbelief, "You want me to wear used clothes?"

With a little grin, "And boots, too. You'll need the costume if you're going to play the part."

Still trying to get back into her bubble, he said, "You know, Legs, I've never had to work this hard to get anything in my life."

"Charlie, let's face it. You've never worked at all, but I still love you. Maybe that's why."

"I don't care why as long as you keep making me happy."

Changing the subject, she asked, "Have you cleaned your trunk out yet?"

"Not yet, why?"

"Never mind. I'll borrow a friend's old work car for the weekend."

Understanding dawned on his face as he said, "Oh, you want us to look poor."

"Right. Now let's go shopping."

Chapter 8

The Gun Show

Even though she had dressed him for the part, Charlie's body language showed he was not comfortable in his surroundings. The one major advantage was no one paid any attention to him. They were both awestruck by the large number of vendors and displays. The show was broken down into categories of guns: historical, hunting, and war.

Looking around she said, "We should be able to find what we need in the war section."

Charlie's attention was drawn to the historical section as a Kentucky rifle captivated him. The gunsmith had created a work of art. The stock was made from a curly maple-stained walnut to showcase the grain. He grabbed her hand and said, "Legs, wouldn't that be beautiful hanging in a Senator's office?"

"We're not here to buy decorations. Boys and their toys. How much cash did you bring?"

"I've got $520," showing her the money.

"Look, they want $500 for just that rifle. If you buy that, then we can't get what we came for without leaving a paper trail placing us here. Let's go find the Springfield rifles before you turn redneck on me."

"Let's split up and we can find them faster," he suggested.

After spending about thirty minutes looking Charlie became frustrated. He walked up to a friendly looking vendor and asked if he knew where he might be able to find a couple of Springfield 03 rifles.

Pointing to his left at the row of tables, he said, "If he hasn't sold them the guy down at the far end had a couple this morning."

Charlie approached the booth. "Sir, I'm looking for Springfield's. The guy at the end said you might have some."

"Yeah. I've got two. Someone tried to convert them to hunting rifles and I can't restore them to the quality I prefer. I'm in the military rifle business, not the hunting business."

Charlie asked, "How much do you want for them?"

The vendor placed the rifles in front of him and said, "I want $35 each."

Charlie picked up each of the rifles separately, "What will you take for both?"

"I can let them both go for $60."

Surprised at how quickly he had lowered his price, Charlie said, "I'll give you $50."

The vendor picked up an open box of ammunition, "If you'll make it $55, I'll throw in some shells. It's not a full box, but they are 160 grain and good for hunting."

Charlie put out his hand, "Mister, you've got a deal."

Charlie rushed the transaction and looked around to make sure Legs wasn't nearby. Not seeing her, he moved quickly back to the booth with the Kentucky rifle.

Enjoying bargaining with the vendors he decided he just might get the rifle today. Having made that decision he approached and said, "Sir, that is a beautiful Kentucky rifle. Would you be willing to let it go for $450?"

"Can't go any lower than $475."

Charlie pulled out his wallet and counted out his remaining bills, then added the three quarters in his pocket. "I have $465 and three quarters." He laid the money on the counter. "I really do want that rifle."

Realizing he couldn't squeeze his customer for any more money, the vendor told Charlie, "You've got a deal."

Charlie felt like a kid again. He couldn't wait to show Legs how he had outsmarted these rednecks. Frustrated after searching with no results for his companion, he headed back to the car. Seeing her waiting for him there he began to talk a mile-a-minute about how he had gotten the Kentucky rifle for his future office and the guns they had come for.

A little irritated she shut him up with, "Is anyone going to remember you? Did you sign anything or tell them anything about yourself that they'd remember? I should never have left you alone. We don't have time for you to gloat. Are you sure no one will remember you?"

"Absolutely. No way."

"I hope so. This afternoon you need to take these rifles to the range and make sure they shoot as well as the other one. We're going to need one of them next week."

"I'll do that. Why don't you drop me off there while you're changing cars and I'll zero them in?"

Charlie was getting frustrated with the new rifles he had just acquired. No matter how hard he concentrated every shot group was at least six inches across. Adding to his aggravation was the fact that he had not kept the rifle butt tight against his shoulder and he was now suffering from multiple bruises. All of this had stolen his macho attitude towards the task at hand. He just wanted to quit and go home, but if he did that, how would he explain to Legs why he hadn't gotten the job done? Then he had an idea. He would ask the owner of the range to do it for him. However, that wouldn't work, as he had no money on him. He approached the elderly gentleman in the lane next to him and described his problem.

"Sir, I've been trying to zero this weapon for more than an hour and I can't even get the shot group small enough to make an adjustment. Can you tell me what I'm doing wrong?"

"Sure, I'd love to. Let me see it for a second."

After looking at the rifle he said, "Here's your problem. Someone has damaged your rear sight. See how loose it is? Every time it's fired the sight moves."

"Can it be fixed?"

"I don't think so. You'll need to replace it or get a gunsmith to fix this one. How long have you had the gun?"

"I just bought it this morning at the gun show."

"You've been screwed," said the man.

"What do you mean?"

"Those gun traders take in a lot of damaged weapons that they could never sell in their store. Their solution is to dump them on the unsuspecting buyers at the gun shows. I'd be willing to bet you he threw in a box of shells, too, didn't he? Just to ease his conscience."

"That's exactly what the son-of-bitch did. Do you think it's worth fixing?"

"If I were you, I wouldn't waste any more money."

Charlie worried. *How am I going to prevent Legs from finding out I screwed up?* Then it came to him. He could use the good rifle for long shots and the others for close ones. He smiled to himself. *How's that for problem solving?* He couldn't wait to be a Senator so he could show the whole state how smart he was. He looked up and saw his car pull into the parking lot. He quickly moved his equipment down two stations so they would be alone when she approached. Still wearing her tight jeans Legs had the attention of every man on the range.

"How's it going?" she asked.

"I'm almost finished. Could you get me two of those 180 gram bullets from the trunk so I can make a final check?"

"Sure, I'll be right back."

Legs saw the men follow her with their eyes and began to exaggerate her hip motion. All the attention was making her excited. She thought to herself, *I still have it.*

Red-faced, Charlie said, "You did that deliberately."

Showing a surprised look on her face, Legs tried to sound innocent. "What?"

"Shaking your ass in front of those men."

"Aw, sweetie, it turns me on to see them get excited and you know you always get the rewards. Do you really want me to stop?"

"Well, if it's only me that gets the reward…."

In a serious voice she broke the spell. "Here are your shells. What are you going to do with them?"

Charlie still wanted to stay on track. "Nothing. Let's go home. I'm too horny to shoot anymore. I'm ready for my reward."

They quickly loaded the equipment and left the range.

Chapter 9

An Upset Father

Monday morning in the Gibson's house Ben walked into Ray's room and shook him awake.

"Get up."

"Huh? What time is it?"

"Eight o'clock. Time all working men are on the job," Ben answered.

"I don't have to work. We're rich."

"All your running around has to stop and it's going to stop today," shouted Ben.

Still half asleep, "What are you talking about?"

"Have you been in Ringgold messing with high school girls?"

Ray looked sick. "Who said so?"

"It looks like you got another girl pregnant, but this time her father wants to either kill you or have you put in jail. He wants us to meet him at the sheriff's office this morning. Did you know the girl you were messing with is only 17 years old?"

"She said she was 23."

"You fool! How many 23 year olds go to high school? I give up. I just don't know what to do with you. Maybe going to jail for a while would be the best solution."

The father finally had his son's attention. Ray felt sick from both the threat of prison and the previous night's drinking. He began to vomit uncontrollably.

Looking up with vomit running down his chin, Ray said, "Daddy, you wouldn't do that to me. What would Mother say?"

With watery eyes, he said, "Truthfully, I think she feels the same way I do. Do you know your mother doesn't even go to social events anymore because you are an embarrassment to her? You have screwed half the daughters of her friends and made it known to anyone who'd listen."

Wiping his chin, Ray begged, "Tell me what to do. I'll do it, I promise. I'll change today."

With fire in his eyes, Ben asked, "How many times have you told me that before?"

"This time I really mean it."

"Okay. Prove it. I don't need words, I need actions. I'll give you a week to find a job. As long as you have a job, you can stay here. If and when you lose that job, you are no longer my son and I will never give you another penny. Is that fair enough?"

"How about you give me a job at the mill?"

"No way. You need to find your own job. It's time you started earning your keep. You need to get out into the world and find out just how hard life really is. When I came to Dalton I didn't have ten dollars. Now, look at what I've achieved."

Ray reversed his approach and lashed out at his dad. "You may fool these mountain people around here but I know you got all your money when you married Mother. Grandpa gave you that first carpet mill. Grandpa told me he even had to run the mill for the first two years to keep you from bankrupting it. You've told this same lie so long that you've actually started to believe it. Crawl down off that cross; you're not fooling anybody."

Ben's face flushed a bright red. He hadn't known that his son knew the true story of his success. When his life's story was expressed in such a demeaning way he was speechless. He just yelled, "Damn you."

As he left the room he repeated, "Get a job!" and slammed the door.

Chapter 10

A Plan Comes Together

Legs pulled Charlie into her arms to keep him at ease. "You've been watching that house for a week and a half now. What have you learned?"

"It looks like Ray leaves every morning around 7:30. Ben leaves exactly at 7:50 a.m. every day and comes home at exactly 4:47 p.m. Ben's wife stays home on Monday, but goes someplace at 9:00 a.m. every Tuesday and Thursday and comes home about 7:00 p.m. On Wednesday she leaves at 1:00 p.m. and comes home around 10:00 p.m."

"Sounds like a family in a rut."

"Not Ray. He always leaves around 7:30, but comes home after his mother leaves. Best part, he's been bringing a woman with him. They both leave just before his Dad gets home."

Releasing Charlie, Legs took a seat at the breakfast bar. "I wonder where he goes every morning."

"Howard Johnson's. I'm beginning to think that's where he picks up his women."

Interested, Legs asked, "How do you know that?"

Expanding his chest, he said, "I followed him a couple of times."

Jumping off the stool, "Did he see you?"

"No, he's only looking for women."

"Is it his girlfriend he brings home, or just a quick lay?"

Not understanding the question, he tried to change the subject. "I love it when you talk dirty."

Annoyed, she demanded, "Answer the question."

"I think they all must be town sluts because it's always a different one. He has only brought one waitress home twice."

She snapped, "Two times in a row or spaced out?"

"Spaced out. What difference does it make?"

Placing her hand on her chin, she replied, "If he's just looking for a quick lay, maybe I can be one of his dates."

Charlie couldn't control his anger. "No! No way. I don't want you screwing anybody else."

She thought *Weak men are all alike.* "Charlie, I love you, but we're not married yet. Can you think of a better way of getting into the Gibson house? Remember, the plan is for you to kill him anyway. The thought of you killing him with his clothes off gets me hot just thinking about it."

Back to his meeker voice, he said, "You're just going to pretend. You're not really going to sleep with him, are you?"

Legs pulled Charlie to her breast. "How else am I going to make it look like his father found him screwing someone right under his own nose?"

Charlie begged, "Can't we do that without you actually doing it with him?"

"You let me handle that part. You just be outside when I open the front door."

Giving him her most alluring smile, she said, "Charlie, all this talk has gotten me hot. Do you think you can do something about it?"

Charlie responded as she expected. As he lifted her she thought, *I wonder if men ever stop being controlled by their hanging down parts?*

Chapter 11

Second Phone Call

"It's time to make your second call to Mr. Gibson."

Charlie timidly asked, "What do you want me to say?"

"Don't worry. Just read this script and be sure you make these points. If you do it right, we should be finished by next week."

With some of the blood coming back to his face, he said, "Then we can get on with making me a Senator."

"Be patient. You're going to be a Senator for a long time. We've got to do this right so no one will suspect you. Here's the phone. Call him."

When the phone was answered, Charlie said, "This is me. Do you have the money together?"

Ben answered in a very low voice, "Yes. I also talked to the doctor."

Charlie read from Legs' list, "We don't need your doctor. I found one in Chattanooga. We plan on leaving town as soon as we get the money."

Charlie could hear the relief in Ben's voice. "What do you want me to do with it?"

Still reading from the list, he said, "I don't want to even see you. I want you to put it in a paper bag with your note and place it in the newspaper box under your mailbox on Tuesday morning. I will pick it up on our way out of town. Is that clear?"

Barely audible, Ben answered, "Yes."

"Gibson, if the money isn't there, expect a family funeral real soon. Do you understand? Otherwise, your troubles with me and my daughter will be over by next weekend." Then he hung up.

"Charlie, you did great." Legs cooed, " You sounded like a really mean bastard. I'll bet Gibson thinks you're a 250 pound redneck who loves to hurt people."

She could see Charlie swell with pride at her comments. She was in control.

Seeking more praise Charlie asked, "You really think so?"

"I know so. Are you ready to finish the job?"

At that moment he felt indestructible. "I'm ready."

"Good. Let's put the equipment in the car."

She went over the plan with him once again. "Your part is really very simple, Make sure you put on your gloves, then with the rifle and three bullets, hide near the front door. I'll open it when I'm ready. Then you need to quickly enter the house and shoot Ray. We'll wait until Ben returns and then you'll kill him. You'll need to place one bullet in Ben's hand and don't forget to put the note with one of his pens on a table near his body."

Charlie grinned, "I get it. The third bullet is for Mrs. Gibson. The bullet and note will make it look like a suicide, won't it?"

Legs agreed. "That's what we want at first."

This caught him off guard. "I don't understand."

"Remember the serial killer that always tried to make his killings look like suicides."

Pleased that he understood he answered, "Oh. I see. You want everyone to think he's back."

"Not yet, but a little later I do. When we take care of the others."

His confidence building, he hugged her. "Sweetie, you're so smart."

"No, I just know what I want."

Concerned, he said, "You mean what we want, don't you?"

Smiling she answered, "No. What I want. I want to marry a Senator. Do you know a Senator who could handle a sexy blonde?"

Chapter 12

Plan's First Step

The sound of loud banging jolted Charlie from sleep Tuesday morning. Staggering to open the front door he was greeted by his angry companion. "Why did you put the chain on? You gave me a key, but it doesn't do any good if you attach the chain. You were still asleep, weren't you?"

Rubbing his eyes, he admitted, "Yeah. What time is it?"

"Six o'clock. We've got to get on the road if we are going to get everything done today. I would like to be gone before Juanita gets here. I'm glad we already loaded the car. Get dressed. Today you take your first step towards being a Senator."

He was so tired he only wanted to go back to bed. He hadn't fallen asleep until almost 4 a.m. He kept worrying that he might screw up. Maybe he would feel better after a shower.

While he was adjusting the water flow she called, "We don't have time for you to primp and strut in front of the mirror. Get a move on."

They were finally on the road. He could tell her patience was wearing a little thin. She kept repeating what they needed to do.

"When we get there you drop me off at Howard Johnson's. Then go to where you can watch the house and mailbox. When you see Ben put the money in the box just wait to get it until his wife leaves. Make sure it's all there and that he didn't forget the note. If it is all there, then hang the red sweater on the mailbox post. That will let me know the plan is working. Do you have any questions?"

When he started to answer her he really looked at her for the first time. He was shocked. "You're not going in there like that are you? I can see your nipples through that blouse. What kind of skirt is that? I don't like this one little bit. "

Her tone changed quickly. "Sweetie, we went over this the other day. I'm just playing a part, remember? Do you think he'll turn me down when I suggest we go to his house?"

Charlie couldn't believe this woman was his, his reply just jumped out, "I don't know how anyone could."

"Great, then you just watch the house and after we've been there for about twenty minutes put on your gloves and follow the plan. Be at the front door when I open it."

He just had to ask, "You're not really going to screw him, are you?"

"You let me worry about that. You just be at the door when I need you."

Looking anxious, he said, "I'm not sure about this."

Eager to get started, she snapped, "I thought you really wanted to be a Senator. If you've changed your mind, just turn the car around and let's go home."

The threat had the effect she wanted.

"No, I want it; I just don't want him touching you."

"Charlie, you need to eat a lot of dirt in this world to get what you want. Now, are we going to do this or not?"

Seeing that she was pissed he answered, "Yeah. But I don't like it."

It was 7:25 a.m. when they drove into Howard Johnson's parking lot. As she got out of the car, she said, "Wish me luck. I'll see you in a couple of hours. Relax and do what we planned. Where's the red sweater?"

"Right here on the front seat."

Talking Rock

"If I don't see the sweater, I'll know he didn't pay the money. I'll have Ray bring me back here. If he didn't do as we said, come back here and wait. Do you have any questions on what you need to do?"

"No. Don't worry, you've gone over it a hundred times."

"Good. Let's go make some money."

When she entered the restaurant, she took the first stool and ordered coffee and toast. She started getting a little nervous from the anticipation of what was about to happen. Then she heard the waitress call, "Morning, Ray. What are you up to?"

"About 5 ft. 8 in. and growing. Where's Maria?"

"She's off. Her kid's sick. You'll just have to put up with me."

"That's okay with me. What will your boyfriend say?" he asked.

She smiled. "I guess I'd better just take your order."

Legs thought, *This is perfect. I don't think Ray will ever recognize me as a blonde.* Moving off the stool and taking her coffee with her she slid into the booth next to Ray and asked, "Are you the famous Ray Gibson?"

With a big smile he responded, "It depends on what you've heard."

She leaned over and whispered in his ear, "You have a big dick and know what to do with it."

He was shocked at first. He only thought men talked like that. He was immediately aroused. "I think so. Why do you ask?"

"Let's just say I'm either a sex-starved housewife or a mature woman who might teach you a thing or two. Which one do you want?"

With his best smile, he replied, "I could learn more."

"You're on, big boy. Where?"

"Let's have breakfast and then go to my place. You know my name. What's yours?"

Pleased that he showed no sign of recognizing her, she answered, "Linda."

"Linda, do you know I can see your nipples through that shirt?"

"Really?" She knew then that he was still just a horny rich kid. Again she was in complete control and loved the feeling of power it gave her.

As they turned into his driveway, he commented, "It looks like one of those kids left their sweater on my mailbox. Remind me to get it when we leave."

"I will. Is all this yours?"

He smiled. "It will be some day."

She thought to herself, *In your dreams.*

When they arrived he almost ran to the door, unlocked it, then rushed to her. "Hurry. I want my first lesson."

"Your first lesson is to be patient. I didn't come here for a wham bam, thank you ma'am fuck. I can get that at home."

"Sorry about that. You're in charge."

"That's good. You're about to feel some excitement you've never felt before."

He began breathing faster. "Promise?"

"Absolutely. Lead the way."

When they got to his bedroom, he turned to her and said, "What are you going to teach me first?"

She opened her purse and pulled out a pair of handcuffs, saying, "To obey."

He opened the top drawer of his nightstand and threw another pair on the bed. "I've played this game before."

With a big smile she said, "I bet you don't know my way of ending the game."

He stripped and jumped on the bed. "Show me."

A feeling of supreme power engulfed her. Knowing what was in store for him caused her to be aroused beyond her expectation. She quickly decided to take total advantage of the situation. It had been a long time since she had had sex for herself only. She had him lay spread-eagled on the bed and cuffed each hand to opposite sides of the headboard. She began a slow strip until he was erect. She pulled out a condom and put it on him. Annoyed, he said, "I thought you wanted the real thing."

"I do. I just don't want to take anything home with me, if you know what I mean."

Talking Rock

She mounted him for the ride of his life. When she was satisfied he had given his all, she quickly dressed. He objected that she still had him handcuffed. She answered, "I'm not through with you. We do have all day, don't we?"

With a puzzled look, he said, "I thought you climaxed. Were you just faking it?"

"Not this time, but unlike you men, we can have more than one. I want my share, is that okay?"

He liked what she was saying and doing. "I'm in your hands, baby."

"I know." She turned and walked to the door.

"Where are you going, baby?"

Turning in the doorway, she replied, "Relax. I have a surprise for you."

She walked slowly out of the room and went downstairs to open the front door. Charlie was waiting. He looked pale and afraid. She saw the fear in his face and wondered if he had the nerve to follow through. "He's in the bedroom at the top of the stairs. He's handcuffed to the bed. All you need to do is shoot him. Make sure you hit him in the middle of his chest. Are you okay?"

Just barely audible, he replied, "I think so."

She could see he didn't have the stomach for this. Panic hit her. She was losing control quickly. Pulling him to the stairs she began saying things to get him mad. "Don't you want to see the bed where he screwed me? He's still there. You can compare dicks."

She could see her comments were having the desired effect. He almost ran up the stairs. She just knew she would hear a shot before she got there. However, all she heard was Ray.

"Who in the hell are you? What are you doing in my house?"

When she walked in the room, Ray asked, "Linda, is this your husband? That's it, isn't it? You two are pulling a con. Well, it's not going to work. You won't get a penny from me. Tell your mousy husband he doesn't scare me with that big rifle of his. Let me loose and you two get out of here before I call the police."

She could see all Ray's yelling was draining the fight from Charlie. If she didn't get control again quickly everything she had worked for would be gone.

"Charlie, why are you letting him talk to you like that? Look how little his dick is."

Ray, insulted, screamed, "You didn't think it was so small when you were climaxing and begging me for ..."

He was interrupted by the noise of the rifle exploding. Ray's body jerked and twitched for a few seconds and then he was dead. Charlie just stood there in a trance. She removed the handcuffs, took out a pair of gloves and began to wipe off anything she might have touched. She then removed a pair of small cotton panties from her purse. Emptying the contents of the condom on the crotch of the panties she dropped them between Ray's legs.

She took Charlie by the hand and led him outside. He was still in a daze. "What do we do now?"

"We just wait. Ben won't be home until after four. Where did you park the car?"

Pointing he answered, "Across the road."

She looked around and realized that they were so isolated there was no danger of any witnesses to their presence. "Let's go to your house, get lunch and let me change clothes."

Charlie, looking weak and as scared as Legs had ever seen him, answered, "How can you eat? We just killed a man."

She knew his ego needed a shot in the arm. "You killed him, my macho man. That makes me love you even more. I didn't realize just how strong you were. You'll make a wonderful Senator."

She could see his chest expanding and was pleased to see how quickly he responded. They ate lunch at Charlie's house. Leaving about 2:30 p.m. they arrived back at the Gibson's house just before 4:00 p.m. She parked out of sight of the driveway. Charlie opened the trunk, put on his gloves, picked up a rifle and two shells.

As they walked to the house she asked, "How many shells did you bring?"

He whispered, "Two."

Patting his shoulder, "That's my man."

Inside the house she worked out what Charlie had to do.

"You need to wait in the other room until Ben takes off his coat. That will be your cue to confront him. Make sure the rifle is within six inches of his chest before you fire."

At exactly 4:47 p.m., Ben drove up. Shortly he entered the living room, set his briefcase down and removed his coat, which he threw on the sofa.

Charlie jumped out like a scared rabbit.

Seeing the gun, Ben said, "Sir, I gave you the money you asked for. Don't hurt me."

Behind Charlie, Legs yelled, "Get closer and shoot."

He did as instructed.

She opened Ben's briefcase and removed a couple of pens. "Where's the note?"

Charlie handed it to her saying, "Let's go. Let's go."

"Relax. It's over. All we need to do is finish setting things up. Put the rifle in his hands as if he shot himself. Put the other bullet in his hand. Here's the pen he used." She placed it and the note on the table next to his body. "Lock the door behind us as we leave."

Chapter 13

Reward For A Job Well Done

Exhausted, they fell back in bed. She had never seen him this aggressive and his stamina shocked her. He'd never lasted more than ten minutes before. The killing of Ben Gibson and his son was having a profound effect on Charlie. He was changing from a boy to a man right before her eyes. Creeping into her consciousness was the fear that she would no longer be able to control him.

"I could eat a horse. Let's go get a steak," he said.

"It's almost 11:00 p.m. Where can we go?"

"I don't know, but we'll find a place. Come on."

She stared at him in amazement. Who was this man? She had never seen him so spontaneous. He was beginning to think on his feet and that worried her.

As they were looking for an open restaurant she suggested he go to Howard Johnson's in Dalton the next morning to listen to the local gossip. She couldn't do it herself, as she might be remembered from the day of the murder. He again surprised her by not objecting and saying, "That's a great idea. I bet that's all they'll be talking about. Every cop in town comes by there for coffee."

It almost sounded like he craved recognition for his achievements.

"Make sure you don't ask any questions or draw attention to yourself. Just listen."

"I know. I'm not stupid. What are you going to do while I'm gone?" he asked.

"I do work for a living, remember. I'll see you this weekend. Our next step is to find another couple to kill, if we're going to make this look like a serial killer."

With an evil grin he asked, "When do I get to take out my uncle?"

"We should wait at least six months to off the Senator if we're going to do this right."

"That's the end of the year. It'll be midway through my uncle's term in office. I know I'd be a shoe-in for his replacement to complete his term." He liked the time frame. Laughing he said, "Incumbents are always reelected here in Georgia. I can't see how I can lose."

She didn't like his use of the word *I* when he talked about being a Senator. Listening to him now, she realized she would have to change her approach and let him think he was making the decisions. Being able to control him without his knowledge could be challenging but nothing she couldn't handle. But increased planning and manipulation might be just what she needed to make this happen. If nothing else, it should be more fun.

Chapter 14

New Revenge

Senator Webb came storming out of his office. "When did you get this package from Coleman?"

His secretary answered, "It was in the morning mail, sir. Is something wrong?"

"I'll say. He's resigned as Brent's attorney. Get Bill Long over here. I want to see him before noon."

Having only seen her boss this angry one other time, she knew to do exactly as he said. He was used to getting his way and if he didn't, things only got worse. She knew he wouldn't settle down this time until he felt Jim Coleman had paid for the slight. It took six phone calls to track down Mr. Long, the investigator. Even though he was in the middle of a critical case, she convinced him it would behoove him to adhere to the Senator's request. Knowing his career would be over otherwise, he was in the office shortly before noon. He had bragged to his friends many times that Webb was not a man to cross as he would not stop until he destroyed anyone threatening his power.

"Long, I want you to find out everything you can about James Coleman, a lawyer in Blue Ridge. Don't come back until you have the kind of information I need. You know what to do."

Trying to keep his voice strong, Long said, "Yes, sir, I do. When do you want it?"

"Yesterday. Don't do any other business until I get what I need. Do I make myself clear?"

"Clear as branch water. Do you have anyone I should contact first?"

"No. I didn't even know about the man until my son got in trouble."

Trying to be helpful Long asked, "Do you want my help on your son's case?"

"No, just find something on Coleman."

The Senator stood there for a minute. "Wait, I take that back. Do you still have that file on Judge Edwards in Cobb County?"

"Yes sir. I can send it over to you by courier before 2:00 p.m."

"Good. I expect you back by the end of the week with the info I need on Coleman. Now get out." The Senator closed the door as Long left.

Chapter 15

The Plan Worked

The following Saturday Legs pumped Charlie about the Gibsons. "What did you find out in Dalton?"

With a gleam in his eye and a smile on his face, Charlie went into his rehearsed speech, "It went just like we planned. The wife found them that night and called the police. They are investigating it as a murder/suicide. One cop told the waitress at Ho Jo's it was good Mrs. Gibson was late coming home because Ben had another bullet in his hand. He figured that one was going to be used to kill her. Basically, they think Ben caught Ray with an underage girl and just snapped."

"What about the missing girl?" she asked.

The question caught him off guard. "I don't think they're looking for her."

She asked, "Why would you think that?".

Charlie tried to defend his thought. "I heard that the sheriff is afraid of what he'll find. I bet he will never pursue it unless someone comes forward. They've already released the bodies and the funerals are set for Sunday."

Surprised she asked, "Tomorrow?"

"Yeah. Everyone I heard talking about it acted like it was expected. Some even commented they thought he should have done it years ago."

"This is better than I expected. We need to check back again in a couple of weeks."

Looking like a proud little boy he asked, "Hey, how are you doing on finding us another target?"

"I thought I had one when I discovered a couple of brothers that are making a killing in the chicken business. Their relationship with their father is what got my attention. The old man won't even speak to them. The bet is when the father dies they won't even attend the funeral. I feel sorry for the old man."

Charlie tried to sound cool. "Do you want to kill both sons?"

"Maybe someday. However, we have to keep focused on our real target – the Senator. I was thinking your uncle knows people all over the state. Is there some way you could find another family that acts like they're royalty and everyone else is there just to serve them?"

"I like that. It would help fit in with our serial killer plot – one of the downtrodden getting even. I'll bet I can get you a long list."

"While you're doing that, you need to start buttering up your aunt. Her endorsement could help you get appointed to fill his position until you can be elected on your own."

"I know just the way."

"How?" she asked.

"I'm the best estate lawyer in the state, remember? I have just six months to set her up for life. She came from a poor background, so I think she'll really appreciate my efforts to not let her slide back into poverty after his death."

"How can you do that without it looking suspicious?" she asked.

"Our law office is a partnership. There's an insurance agent that has tried for years to sell us key-man insurance in case of one of the partners' deaths. The Senator has said no in the past, but I have always been in favor of it. I'll approach him about it again and tell him of my concern that the business would fall apart without him. His ego will do the rest."

"I like it. How long do you think it'll take?"

"Not more than a month," he replied.

"Then we'll just be patient. Where did you put the money?"

Charlie just stood there with a blank expression on his face.

She screamed, "My God! Tell me you didn't lose it."

Charlie stuttered and finally stammered out, "I think it's still in the back seat of the car."

Running to the door she said, "Let's go check."

Sure enough, the money was lying right where Charlie had tossed it. She seized the bag and pulled it tightly to her breast. "We've got to find a safe place for this."

Trying to be helpful Charlie offered, "I have a wall safe in my office."

"Does anyone else use it?'

"No, in fact I haven't used it in years."

Smiling reassuringly, she said, "Perfect. Put the money in the safe and leave it alone for a couple of years."

Surprised, he said, "Years? Why so long?"

"Just a precaution, in case the bank marked the bills."

Pleased with her answer, he smiled, "You're always thinking."

"It's a good thing or you'd have us in jail." She walked away thinking to herself, *I swear you're going to be the death of us.*

Chapter 16

A Senator's Wrath

Bill Long was nervous about the meeting. He had some information, but nothing close to what the Senator was expecting to hear. He had long ago learned not to defend himself when presenting what he had. The Senator was a very impatient man, just looking for the bottom line. Reading from his notebook seemed to be the best approach as the Senator usually listened while he was reading. However, when he stopped, he knew if what he had wasn't sufficient there would be hell to pay.

He began with his summary: "Jim Coleman moved to Blue Ridge more than ten years ago. He was the husband of Margaret 'Peggy' Taylor, who was executed for the double murder of her father and brother. He has a son born while Taylor was in jail. After her death, he worked at the Blue Ridge Post Office and went to night school and began to practice law almost five years ago. He now has an office in Blue Ridge with an ex-Georgia State patrolman working as his Private Investigator. He and his son live with an elderly couple, Michael and Martha Barkley, who once ran the post office. He is a wealthy man; however, I can't determine where the money came from--maybe from his son's trust. That's all I have so far." He stood with a dry mouth expecting the worst.

The Senator surprised him by only saying, "I remember the Taylor case. She killed Bob and Craig Foster. You may be right about the trust.

Bob Foster was the richest man I ever knew. He had a brother who was a judge in Fannin County, didn't he?"

"Yes, sir, he did."

He snapped, "Is he still in office?"

"No, sir, without his brother's help he was voted out of office."

"Then I think Judge Foster just might be Coleman's Achilles heel. Find him and bring him to me, but not here." Pacing as he thought about the best solution he said, "Bring him to my house."

"When do you want to see him?"

"Let's do it this weekend. You set it up and tell Foster to keep his mouth shut if he knows what's good for him. That goes for you, too. Now get out of here."

About one o'clock on Sunday afternoon, Long had the Judge in tow.

Wondering why he was there, Judge Foster followed Bill Long up the long driveway to Senator Webb's home. Since they had only met twice previously at political fundraisers, he couldn't imagine any reason he might have been summoned. As he pondered possibilities, it occurred to him that perhaps there was hope of the Senator helping him regain a judgeship if he were able to assist him in whatever he needed. The housekeeper ushered him out to the pool where the Senator was waiting. Looking around to be sure their conversation would be private, the Senator got right to the point. "Do you know Jim Coleman?"

Caught off guard, Foster said, "Why, yes. He was married to my niece."

"How do you feel about him?"

Foster began to tell the tale of how he and his wife had tried to adopt Coleman's son, who came with a sizeable inheritance. As he relayed the events, his temper and frustration in the situation became obvious. The Senator smiled with pleasure at Foster's outrage and hatred of Coleman. He sensed he had an ally in his plan to ruin the lawyer. Foster quickly realized by assisting the Senator in getting the results he wanted, there would be much to gain. He immediately volunteered information as to what he thought was Jim's weak spot. "I think the thing that would hurt him the most would be if you could somehow take his son away from him."

"And you and your wife could help me by playing Mommy and Daddy?" The Senator had meant the remark to be sarcastic; however, once he said it out loud he realized it had potential. Realizing they may have hit on a solution he said, "How can we make this happen? Does Coleman have any powerful friends?"

Foster nodded, "Yes, right now he does. However, with a little help from a friend, that could change."

"Who's the friend? Can he be trusted?"

"Clay Cagle. He was a deputy sheriff in Fannin County, and Jim Coleman got him fired. He will do anything to pay him back."

In a lower voice, the Senator asked, "Will he have trouble bending the law a little?"

"Bending the law is what got him fired. I almost went down with him. He owes me big time. If you don't mind me asking, what did Coleman do to you?"

Not liking the question the Senator said, "It's not me. He refused to help my son who's in trouble over a fight in school. They've also trumped up charges that a witness saw him selling drugs. Coleman just wanted him to plead guilty. If he did that, my career would be over. The media would have a field day."

"Would I be presumptuous by asking if you're looking for someone else to represent him?"

Impressed, the Senator asked, "Are you asking for the job?"

"I think I could settle this without it ever going to court. How badly hurt is the kid he fought?"

"He's still in the hospital with major cuts on his face, which will require plastic surgery."

With authority, Foster asked, "Do you think the parents can afford that?"

"No. They're just cotton farmers. That's why they're pressing it."

Foster suggested, "What if you offered to cover all of the costs up to, say, $100,000? But only if they drop the charges and keep their mouths shut."

Liking what he heard, the Senator smiled, "Yeah. That's a lot of money for a farmer. Let's start with $50,000. That might work. But what about the witness?"

"Let's let Cagle take care of this witness. That should remove your doubts about him. I'll let Clay know that his success with this task would determine how much support he could get with Coleman. I don't think I should let him know who you are just yet."

The Senator really liked how Foster thought, "I agree, and it has to be quick. Brent's case comes before the grand jury in less than four weeks."

"That's close, but I think we can make it happen. I recommend we postpone any plans for Coleman until we get your son cleared."

Nodding his agreement the Senator said, "I'm in no rush. I want to see him twist and turn."

Handing Foster a beer he said, "Here's to a new, productive partnership."

"Here, here!"

Chapter 17

The Witness

Paul Manwaring couldn't believe his luck. He was in his favorite bar, getting ready to hustle the biggest sucker he'd hooked in quite a while. His mark was a rich young man, as usual, who had come to slum and show the locals he was better than they were. Their only redeeming quality was they came with lots of money. After counting the $250 in his pocket he realized he needed to engage this one before another local took him away. They'd already played for two hours and Paul had let him win two games by scratching the eight-ball. This guy would be good for at least another $250 if he played his cards right. His date could wait. The sex she offered couldn't compare with the thrill of walking away with over $500 for the night. This guy really liked his liquor. He kept ordering new rounds before they had even finished the ones they had.

Getting ready to make his move, he decided to distract the guy with small talk. "If I'm going to get drunk with you and take your money, you could at least tell me your name."

Clay Cagle quickly responded with a fake name. "Troy. Is it my break?"

"Sure. Mine's Paul."

"Paul, you sure have been lucky tonight."

"It's better to be lucky than good any day."

"You're right. What about doubling the stakes? Your luck has to run out sometime."

Thinking, *There's no luck here, just a poor player,* he laughingly agreed.

By midnight Paul had accumulated $650 of Troy's money. He decided to up the stakes again. "Troy, let's play one last game for $100."

"Okay, it is getting late. You break and I'll get us another round."

While Paul was busy, Clay discreetly dropped something into the drink before handing it to him.

Dawn was just breaking as Paul was dropped onto a blanket spread on the ground. Disoriented, he realized his hands and feet were tied and there was a foul smell in the air. Looking anxiously at the man in front of him, he asked, "Why am I tied like this? Where am I?"

"You sure have a lot of questions. You're in a graveyard."

"Graveyard? It smells like a garbage dump."

"That's what I said. This dump is your graveyard."

The blood drained from Paul's face as he weakly asked, "You're going to kill me?"

"That's the plan. You pissed off some important people."

Pleading, Paul said, "You can't kill me. I didn't do anything."

"Not yet you haven't, but you will. That's why I have to kill you. I didn't realize how much work it was going to be or I wouldn't have taken the job."

"What kind of work?"

"I have to kill you and then bury your body in the middle of this dump so you won't be found."

Realizing what this had to be about, all the blood drained from Paul's face. "Wait. Does this have to do with Brent? What if I left the state and didn't return?"

Manipulating this kid was going to be easier than he thought. He just needed to put a little more pressure on him to ensure he would disappear. Realizing he was in complete control, he played along, enjoying every minute.

Talking Rock

Clay asked, "Where would you go?"

Grasping at any solution Paul quickly suggested, "I've got kin in Oklahoma."

"Do you think the sheriff is stupid? Your relatives would be the first place they'd look, especially those out of state. What about someplace your family wouldn't know about?"

"Yeah, I've got a friend in Texas. We were busted together. He went to jail and I got probation because I was underage. He owes me big. Because I wouldn't testify against him his sentence was a short one."

"I think we may be onto something here. Are you sure no one knows about this guy?"

"Absolutely. My family can't stand him. They think he's still in jail."

Clay asked, "Okay. How do we handle your family?"

"There's only Mom and my little brother. All I need to tell them is that I'm in trouble again and need to run."

"Do you think they'll turn you in?"

"No. Mom's no fan of the police. Daddy used to beat her and they wouldn't help."

Clay suggested, "Let's find a pay phone and I'll see how well you do."

Clay listened to the kid handle his family, "Kid, with a performance like that you should be an actor. Are you playing a game with me? If you are it's just a short drive back to that dump. Let me make this simple for you. If either my partner or I see you anywhere in the state of Georgia your Mom will get your head in the mail. Do you doubt I'll make that happen?"

With a tremor in his voice, Paul said, "No, sir."

"Good. Then I'm driving you to Atlanta to the bus station and buying you a one-way ticket to Texas."

Clay handed Paul the money he had taken off him while he was unconscious. "Use this to buy a ticket to whatever town you need once you get to Texas."

"I need to stop by my house and get some clothes."

"I knew I was making a mistake to trust you. It's only been five minutes and you're already changing the rules."

Scared, Paul apologized, "I'm sorry. I wasn't thinking."

"How many times between here and Texas are you not going to think?"

Paul promised, "I'll keep my mouth shut, honest."

"That's it. I want you to act like you're dumb until you get to Texas."

"You mean retarded?"

"No. You're already retarded, stupid. Dumb means you can't talk."

Clay left the car and went to the pay phone pretending to make a call. When he returned he said, "My friend will be on that bus with you. If he sees you talking to anyone, he'll stick a knife in you and throw you in a ditch at the next stop. Do you understand?"

"I won't talk to a soul. I promise. You'll see."

"My partner will see."

An hour later, watching the bus pull out of the station, Clay was proud of his idea of telling Paul he had someone watching him on the bus. He laughed out loud realizing Paul would be suspicious that anyone who looked at him could be his killer. He couldn't wait to tell Judge Foster what he had done. This should prove to Foster's friend that he could get the job done.

Chapter 18

The Boys Are Back In Court

While Jim and Sam were discussing the week's activities, Shirley came in with the appointment book and said, "I thought I'd remind you. It's been a year since Johnny and Doug were put on probation. They need to report back to the Judge."

Amazed, Jim said, "Already? You're kidding me."

Sam smiled. "Jim, time flies when you're having fun."

"See when Sue can come in. Sam, you're going to take care of Doug, aren't you?"

"That's what I promised the Judge."

Nodding, Jim said, "See what day works for the Judge, Shirley. We'll just need an office visit. Sam, when was the last time you talked with that couple that Johnny and Doug burglarized?"

"Mr. and Mrs. Gray? I saw them last week. They couldn't be happier. The boys cut and trim their yard about every 10 to 12 days. To tell you the truth I think Doug has adopted them as grandparents. Would you believe they have pictures of the boys on their mantel?"

"Sam, you make it sound like a story book ending."

"It does sound a little corny, doesn't it?"

"Let's just hope it's not too corny for the Judge," said Jim.

Later that day Shirley stuck her head in Jim's office, "The Judge is available on Thursday at four-thirty."

"Why so late?"

"I reminded his clerk that Sue was a teacher and a single parent."

Smiling, Jim said, "Shirley, what would I do without you? I'll need to see Sue, Johnny, Doug and Sam sometime before we go see the Judge."

"They'll be here this afternoon at five."

Jim shook his head, "When is the last time I sent you flowers?"

Winking, she said, "Do you want me to take care of that, too?"

"You're worse than Mother. I can never get the best of her either."

At five Jim walked into the conference room and saw that everyone was there. Johnny and Doug looked as if they would pass out if he spoke to them.

He got straight to the point. "Hi, folks. I'm sure Shirley has told you that Judge Colwell will talk with the boys on Thursday. Sue, how is Johnny doing?"

She smiled and said, "He's been wonderful. He had a B+ average for the school year and he and Doug have started a lawn mowing business this summer."

"That's great. I know that's what the Judge will want to hear. Sue, how's life at home with you and the boys?"

"We're fine."

Moving closer to Sue so the boys couldn't hear, Jim asked, "Are the boys' grandparents helping you out now?"

Speaking softly, she replied, "No, they still treat us like we have the plague, but the boys have really helped with their business."

Chapter 19

A Pact

Clay Cagle reported back to Judge Foster like a well-trained retriever. He was looking for the same reward a good bird-dog would seek-- praise. He was disappointed. Judge Foster's only comment was, "Good. Now there's no witness. No witness. No case. Those Earlys couldn't cash that check fast enough. I'll bet you ten to one that kid never sees another doctor, let alone a plastic surgeon." Thinking out loud, he said, "Now I just have to talk with the prosecutor and have the charges against Brent dropped."

In order to get Foster's attention, Clay asked, "Do you think your friend will be pleased enough to help me hurt Coleman now?"

"I'm sure he'll help, but one favor won't be enough for him to cash in any big chips."

"Just tell me what needs to be done. I underestimated that bastard once, but I won't make that mistake again. He's a royal pain in the butt – he and that investigator of his destroyed my perfect record and got me fired."

The judge asked, "Is he that good in court? He never came before me when I was a judge."

Clay answered, "I don't know about that."

"Can you get any dirt on him?"

"What kind of dirt do you want?"

"Something that could end his career or, better still, sends him to jail."

With a satisfied smile, Clay said, "Sounds like you hate him more than I do. Does it have to be completely legal?"

"It only needs to look that way, if you know what I mean."

Nodding yes, he said, "I hear you loud and clear."

"Keep in touch at least once a week. Together I think we can make life a living hell for Jim Coleman."

Sunday afternoon Judge Foster and Senator Webb were having their routine meeting.

"Foster, I'll be the first to admit I underestimated you. Just as you predicted, the case against Brent fell apart. Even the school principal called me to apologize for suspending him. He assured me nothing would be entered into his school records."

With his hands folded in his lap, the judge answered, "Thanks. I'm just glad I could do the favor."

With disbelief, the Senator said, "Are you saying it's free?"

"I'd like to, but my law firm is falling on bad times. I hope you understand."

The Senator laughed, "Just pulling your chain. In fact, you saved me a lot of money and I didn't need to play my chip on a certain Cobb County judge. I can use that for something later. Here's a small check for your services."

Looking at the check the judge was pleased. "Are you sure? This is for $25,000. "

Sounding offended, the Senator asked, "Not enough?"

"Oh no. More than enough."

"I'm glad you're happy. Getting Brent free made my wife happy and that's worth much more. Now it's time for us to get going on the project I wanted you for in the first place – Jim Coleman. How are you doing on that?"

"I was waiting until Brent's case was closed first. I want to put all my attention on Coleman when we start. Cagle is ready and willing."

Walking the floor, the Senator asked, "How long do you think it'll take to get him?"

Cautious as ever, the judge said, "I'm not sure. We can't rush it. We may only get one chance and I don't want to waste it."

Realizing the judge was a little shaken, the Senator said, "I underestimated you once. I won't do that again. You call the shots. I just want him to know you don't mess with this Senator."

His confidence restored, the judge said, "And Judge Foster, too."

Chapter 20

The Next Step

It was later on Saturday night when Charlie heard a knock on his front door. Answering it he asked, "Why didn't you use your key?"

Legs smiled. "It's been so long, I thought you might be mad."

"I am mad. It's been weeks since I've seen you. Not even a telephone call. I thought you were dead or worse."

"What could be worse?"

Looking at the floor, he said, "You not wanting me anymore."

Sighing with relief that she still had power over him, "Oh, don't be silly. I'll show you how much I missed you."

He couldn't get her into bed fast enough. Making love like a loved-starved teenager, he was through in less than ten minutes. Although it ended quickly, she was pleased because now she could get to her real agenda.

He asked, "Where have you been? You could've at least called."

"I did call, but you were never home and I knew I couldn't call you at work."

"Why not?"

"Let's say I felt it would be safer if no one knew about me for a little while longer."

"You still haven't told me where you've been."

Lying she said, "I had an opportunity to help a friend cater a big dinner and I couldn't pass up the extra money."

"Why didn't you tell me? I would have given you the money you need."

"I appreciate the offer, but I don't want to take money like a prostitute."

"Why would you ever think I'd think of you that way? You don't need to be so proud. Accept a little help."

"Pride is the one thing a poor person has to depend on. I know you don't know what I'm talking about so let's just drop the subject. Okay?"

Seeing her in a different light, Charlie said, "You're so independent. I think that's what I love most about you."

Trying to change the subject, Legs said in a business-like voice, "Have you been back to Dalton?"

"Yes, twice, in fact. Would you believe it? I didn't hear one comment about the Gibson's. They all act as if nothing ever happened."

"That's good for now. How are you doing on buttering up your aunt?"

Looking at the floor, Charlie mumbled, "Not so good."

Quickly determining the problem she said, "The Senator still doesn't want to do the life insurance thing?"

"No. That's going quite well. In fact, all the partners have completed their medical evaluations and we should have the policy in hand soon."

Confused, she asked, "Then what's the problem?"

"The Senator and his wife have a new bosom buddy. It's a Judge Foster from Blue Ridge, I think."

"What makes him so special?"

"The Senator's son, Brent, got into some real trouble at school and this guy got the charges dropped. If I hear one more time how wonderful he is, I think I'll puke. What are we going to do? If anything happens to the Senator now, they might make Foster his replacement instead of me."

"We can't have that." Legs said.

"I know, but what are we going to do?"

Talking Rock

She could hear the insecurity in his voice, but what was worse was the look of despair on his face. It was clear to her that Charlie had very little staying power. She was the strong one here and she was beginning to think he might be too weak to do his part of her ambitious plan. One problem at a time. Right now she needed to put her sexual powers to work to remove his fears and increase his self-esteem.

Pulling him into her arms she whispered, "Never mind that now. Just relax and show me again how much you missed me."

When he was in her arms he felt like he could do anything and overcome any obstacle. She could see the change in his demeanor and began to build his ego. Calling him Senator and talking about what a perfect job he had done on the Gibsons was all that was needed to get him ready for the next step of the gruesome plan.

As she put her clothes on she stopped and turned to Charlie. "Are you ready to become a Senator?"

"Yes. But what about Judge Foster?"

In a calm and cool voice, she explained, "We can take care of him when you take care of your uncle"

Confused, Charlie said, "I don't understand."

"I'm talking about killing them both with the same shot. You said you could hit a Coke can at 150 yards. Can you hit two Coke cans six feet apart at 150 yards?"

A smile came across his face at the thought. "I don't know, but I will tomorrow."

"Great. You need to find out where your uncle and judge meet. We need a place where you can make the shot and not be discovered."

"Leave that to me. I should be spending more time with my sweet aunt."

She was pleased to see his reaction to the situation. "One other thing. I need the name of a good investigative reporter with the *Atlanta Journal*."

"That's easy. Bill Dean. He's the best. He has the nickname of 'Bulldog' because once he starts an investigation he won't quit."

"Do you have his telephone number?" she asked.

"At the office."

She cautioned, "Make sure no one sees you get it."

A little angry he barked back, "I know that."

Seeing that she had pushed him too hard she slid into his arms and whispered, "I love it when you get excited."

He reacted, as she knew he would. She just hoped she would always be close by when he had these weak moments.

Chapter 21

The Reporter

During a long lunch break, Legs made a call to Bill Dean. She had located the perfect phone booth where she could not be seen or heard. *The Atlanta Journal* operator answered on the second ring and so quickly connected her that she was caught off guard.

"Mr. Dean?"

"Yes, what can I do for you?"

"No, it's what I can do for you. What's the story of a lifetime worth to you?"

Trying to dismiss her, he said, "This paper is not in the habit of buying news."

"I'm not talking to the paper – I'm talking to you. Are you interested or do I need to find a more ambitious reporter?"

That tweaked his interest. "I need to know more about this story."

"That's fair enough. Would you be interested in knowing there's a serial killer in Georgia? He's been killing for almost 15 years and the authorities keep covering it up."

"If this is true, and you can prove it, it might just be the story of a lifetime."

Now that she had him hooked, she said, "If you're as good as they say you are, you can prove it."

"How do you know all this?"

"I'm the killer's girlfriend."

A little surprised, he asked, "Why are you turning him in now?"

"He wants me to help with his killings, but doesn't want to share any of the money."

"What money?"

"Each time he kills, he gets over $200,000."

"I thought you said he was a serial killer. It sounds more like he's a paid assassin."

"Not really. He kills for revenge after he blackmails them."

Fishing for more information, he asked, "How many people has he killed?"

"Somewhere between 10 and 15. I'm not sure."

"The authorities haven't done anything?"

"He's smart. The killings always look like a murder/suicide or he frames someone else."

Still suspicious, he asked, "Are you sure he's not just a bedroom killer? Just making up big stories to impress you?"

Legs lost her temper and said, "You don't believe me, do you?"

"Do you have any facts to support this outlandish accusation?"

"I'll give you facts. He killed Ben and Roy Gibson in Dalton last winter. He also killed the Fosters in Blue Ridge and framed the daughter. Check it out." Then she abruptly hung up.

A month later, frustrated, Legs threw the newspaper on the table. "Nothing. What do I need to do to get his attention?"

Her oldest looked at her and said, "Mom, what are you talking about?"

"Nothing. I'll be at Charlie's tonight. Here's money for pizza."

They loved for their mother to spend time with Charlie. That meant they could get real food. They had bets with their friends that their mom was the worst cook in the world. Legs had been so focused the past week on finding some sign that Bill Dean was on the trail of the serial killer that she had let her relationship with Charlie cool. This dawned on her when she realized she was at home on a Saturday night. She reminded herself that weak boys need constant attention. She shrugged off the queasy feeling by reassuring herself that an afternoon of heated sex would correct the situation. It was after 6 o'clock when she entered his house. All the lights were out in the front rooms. Calling out for him, she walked towards the back of the house. Hearing a slurred answer she realized he was in the kitchen. There was an almost empty half gallon bottle of vodka sitting in front of him. He was using a water glass to speed up the process of getting drunk.

"Charlie, you're drunk."

Barely able to talk he said, "Yeah, I am. Who cares?"

"I do. I hate to see you like this. You haven't been this drunk since I first met you two years ago. Is it because I didn't come down last night?"

"No. It's my uncle."

"Your uncle? What did he do now?"

"I was spending time with him and my aunt like you suggested. At noon he pulled me aside and told me he had business friends coming and I needed to leave. I waited on the highway next to the driveway and I saw that his meeting was with Judge Foster."

"What's wrong with that?"

"It's the way he made me feel – like a child being sent away while the adults talked. Nothing has changed. I thought with all I had done for the firm with the key man insurance he would have given me a little more respect."

"Charlie, what do you care? He'll be dead in a few months."

Straightening up in his chair he said, "I'll make certain of that. And his bosom buddy Foster, too."

"Let's get you something to eat."

After a meal and a couple of hours, Charlie began to sober up. She asked, "Have you worked out a plan for shooting your uncle and Foster?"

"Yes, I have. But aren't we going to kill another father and son first? To make it look like that serial killer."

"That would take another couple of months, and from what you're saying we can't afford to wait. What's your plan?" she asked.

"There's an old logging road that goes right behind his property. I can park there and no one will see my car. It's only 100 yards to the perfect spot to make the shot. The distance from the ambush site to my uncle's table is 142 yards."

"How do you know that?"

"I bought a range finder a couple of weeks ago."

She smiled. "You really are becoming a macho man." The compliment was not lost on him. She could see his self-esteem improve as he went on describing his plan. "They meet every third Sunday at 13:00."

"You make it sound so military."

The praise was having the desired effect on Charlie.

"I agree it's time to make our move."

"Before we do, could you show me the ambush site next weekend?"

He proudly announced, "I can do that."

Chapter 22

Judge's Chambers

Judge Colwell had the boys sit in straight-back chairs right in front of his desk. The impact was not lost on Doug or Johnny. They were sweating and as pale as corpses. Although there were six people in the office, you could hear a pin drop. Judge Colwell's low speaking voice sounded like thunder to the boys.

"Mr. McGill, what were your grades for the last school year?" he asked.

Sue said, "He had a B plus average."

The judge gave her a cold stare and looked straight at Johnny and said, "The boy can speak for himself. Is that the truth?"

In a small voice he answered, "Yes sir. I had two As."

"And how were your grades?"

In an even weaker voice than Johnny, he said, "I had a B average and I had one A plus."

"What was the A plus in?"

Beaming, Doug said, "Geometry."

With a slight smile the judge asked, "Doug, what are you going to be when you grow up?"

"I'm going to be a helicopter pilot like Mr. Wright."

Switching his attention to Sam, the judge said, "I didn't know you flew helicopters."

"I don't now. I flew lift ships in 'Nam."

"Huey's?"

"Yes, sir, with the 1st Cav Division."

"Johnny, what are your plans for the future?" asked the judge.

Sitting straight in his chair, Johnny answered, "I'm going to be a school teacher like Mom."

The look on Sue's face showed that this was a complete surprise to her. Seeing that, the judge spoke with authority and asked, "Is this the truth or are you boys just saying this to impress me?"

Both boys answered, "Honest, it's the truth. We wouldn't lie to you."

"That's good to hear, but you shouldn't lie to anyone. I'm impressed with you both. These are very ambitious goals and will take a lot of work to make them come true. Are you willing to work that hard?"

Doug was the first to answer. "Yes, sir. I plan to keep my grades up, go to North Georgia College, be a 2nd Lieutenant in the Army and fly helicopters."

Johnny chimed in with, "I'm going to North Georgia to be a teacher."

"I have just one last question. Where do you boys plan on getting the money for college?"

Johnny answered, "That's easy. Doug and I are mowing lawns. We've saved over $600 this summer."

"So you have a lawn mowing business, huh?"

"Yes, sir. Half the money I make goes to Mom and the other half goes into my savings account."

"What do you do with your money, Doug?"

"I give part to my grandparents and the rest goes into my savings account."

Looking at the file, the Judge asked, "What about the Grays? Are they happy with the boys' work?"

Sam said, "I can answer that, sir. They couldn't be happier. Before the boys took on the responsibility of cutting their lawn, the Grays could only afford to have it cut once a month. Doug and Johnny cut and trim it about every ten to twelve days now. But, what I think they really enjoy the most is the boys' company."

Looking up at Sue and Sam, the judge said, "I'm impressed with their progress – so much so that I will expunge their records. I'll expect you both to keep up the great mentoring and I look forward to an invitation to their graduations. Now why don't we all go home for supper?"

Jim spoke, "Thanks, Judge."

He answered, "No thanks needed. You all did the hard part."

Chapter 23

Another Call

Another week went by without any mention of the serial killer. Angry and frustrated, Legs made another call to Bill Dean. When he answered the phone, she screamed at him for how incompetent and useless he was.

When she had vented enough that he could respond he tried to explain that he had checked out the Gibsons and the case had been closed. It was a murder/suicide. That explanation really set her off.

"You stupid bastard. I told you that."

"Listen lady, I'm good at my job. First I have to prove to my editor that you're not a fraud. I get calls like this all the time and they usually don't pan out. Give me something to work with if you expect results. I need details, not hints."

His business-like response seemed to calm her down.

"So you're not just ignoring me?" she asked.

"No, ma'am. If I can prove what you're saying is true it could make me famous. So tell me everything you know, and don't worry; I have never revealed a source."

"Okay. He likes to kill rich people, usually father and son. He always uses an old Army rifle. I think they call it an 03, whatever that means. I do know it shoots a 30-06 bullet because he's always bragging about what a wonderful shot group he has."

"Give me more names," he said.

"Well, I gave you the Gibsons and the Fosters. I don't know names of the others, but I think he killed someone last month. The next time he's drunk I'll get him to tell me. He's proud of the fact that no one has ever suspected they were murdered."

"The Fosters? Are you telling me they executed the wrong person? Now *that* would be a story. Do you have anything else I can work with?" he asked.

"Yeah, he plans to kill somebody else soon and leave the state."

"How soon?" he asked.

"Maybe this fall; he wants to be gone by winter." She abruptly hung up.

Chapter 24

Time To Kill

The third weekend of the month had finally arrived. Charlie was like a little boy on Christmas Eve. There was a special gleam in his eye, one that came from knowing he was about to achieve his lifelong dream. The fact that a man had to die for it had no impact on his enthusiasm. Saturday morning he was up and on the firing range. This was a very special day and he wanted to be there before anyone else. He had planned what he was going to do all week. He was pleased to see he had the entire range to himself. He carried two bags to the firing line and took out two full Coke cans and the range finder. He taped the cans to 1" by 1" stakes. With the stakes, range finder and a hammer he walked straight out from his firing point. When he thought he was about the right distance, he turned and saw through the range finder that he was at 152 yards. He walked back to exactly 142 yards and drove in one stake. Taking three more steps he set up the other stake. He now had the cans lined up for the shot. Hurriedly he returned to the firing line. Placing only one round in the rifle, he knew everything relied on making just one shot. He placed the rifle on the sand bag in front of him. He was excited and a little nervous. He put the crosshairs on the center of the first can. He could just barely see the top of the second. Taking a breath and then letting it out he squeezed the trigger. Both cans exploded from the impact. Quickly he put his gun and equipment back into the two bags. Leaving the two stakes downrange, he drove home. Smiling, he turned the radio to maximum volume while thinking, *I'm ready*.

Legs showed up about 4 o'clock. He excitedly told her about the morning's events. He could think about nothing else. He was in his own little world now and that worried Legs. She had thought he might not be up to the task; after all, it was his uncle. However, it seemed she was a distraction to him. Seeing that he might be better left alone she made up an excuse to return home. Charlie casually raised his hand and said, "See ya tomorrow night."

Sunday morning he drove out to the logging road. He was about to stop when he saw two hunters walk out of the woods. Driving down the road a short distance, he watched as they got into their truck and drove off. He thought to himself, *That's right. It's squirrel season. No one will pay any attention to my gunshots.* He smiled, *This is just too perfect.*

Parking in his predetermined spot he quickly moved to his ambush site. He took a full sandbag from his equipment bag and placed it on a log he had previously moved into place. Then he took out his rifle. Looking in the bag for the ammunition, he discovered he only had two bullets left. He decided that would be okay, as he only needed one. For safety's sake he did put both bullets in the rifle. Now all he had to do was wait.

It was quite a wait. He decided the two hunters had left too early. He had counted over 15 squirrels since they left. Then at 1 o'clock two cars drove up the driveway. He began to have doubts. What if they didn't come outside? What if they saw him first, or what if they never lined up for one shot? As he worried, they opened the back door and walked towards the table. He relaxed a little. Then pure panic slammed him in the gut. There was a third man with them. What was he to do? He sat patiently for about 20 minutes before the third man got up and walked towards the car. Thinking the third guy was leaving he started looking through the scope for the perfect shot. Then it happened.

The Senator offered the judge a beer and they stood up for what looked like a toast. With this movement both targets were lined up just like the Coke cans. He took a deep breath, let it out and squeezed the trigger. It surprised him how loud it sounded in the woods. Both men dropped. Then without warning, dust kicked up in front of him and he heard the sound of a gunshot. Looking at the house he could see the third man running towards him firing a pistol. He froze momentarily until he remembered the second round. He quickly opened the bolt, ejected the empty hull and placed the last round into the chamber. The man was coming straight for him. All he could think of was sighting the crosshairs onto the center of this mad man. The rifle seemed to fire on its own. The man acted as if he had been hit with an invisible baseball bat. Charlie watched for about five minutes and saw no movement from any of the three. He grabbed his equipment and ran to the car.

Chapter 25

A Killing

Sam burst into Jim's office. "Have you heard?"

"What?"

"Judge Foster and Clay Cagle were shot yesterday."

"Were they killed?"

"Yeah, along with Senator Webb from Cartersville."

"*Our* Senator Webb?" asked Sam.

"Yeah. They were all killed at the Senator's house."

"Doesn't it make you wonder what those three have in common?"

"I was thinking the same thing. Do you think they could possibly have any connection to you?"

"I don't think so. We know Foster and Cagle were the masterminds of the child abuse setup that got Cagle fired, but why would the Senator be involved?"

"You did say he was really pissed when you rejected his son's case."

"He was, but I'm not sure he was mad enough to take any kind of action against me."

"You pay me to be suspicious and look at all possibilities, right? This looks mighty suspicious to me," said Sam.

"I'll admit I'm not sad they're dead, but I don't think the killer was thinking of me when he pulled the trigger. They were killed for other reasons. Trust me."

Sam smiled. "I have always known you were born with a horseshoe in your back pocket. You must be living right. "

"I agree things seem to be going my way lately, but don't stop your investigation. Do whatever it takes to find out what you can," directed Jim.

Standing, Sam said, "I'll go down to Cartersville and nose around."

"If you don't mind, update me every time you learn something new."

Two nights later Sam came to Jim's house for his first update. Meeting him at the door, Jim asked, "What did you find out?"

"As you would expect, every police force in the state is involved."

"Do they know who did it?" asked Jim.

"Not yet. They have set up a special task force headed by the GBI. I thought I'd go down to their headquarters next week and talk with Walter Rogers."

"That's a great idea. Do you think he'll actually share info with you?" asked Jim.

"I hope so. All those years we worked together on Peggy's case made us pretty tight. We are friends and since I started work here Walter has been my mentor. We talk every month about how I can improve my investigation work," admitted Sam.

"So, the secret's out. That's how you perfected your skills so quickly," teased Jim.

Sam flinched. Realizing he had hurt Sam's feelings, Jim put his hand on Sam's shoulder and apologized. "That was meant to be a compliment, big guy."

Sam said, "Does that mean I can keep my job?"

"Until you're 80; then we'll talk about how long you can stay."

"You know you're starting to sound like the old, carefree Jim of yesteryears."

"With the child abuse thing gone, I've decided it's time to smell the roses."

"You know, I may need to stay in Atlanta for a few days."

Talking Rock

"Do what you need to. JM and I are trying to move from the lake cabin to Mike's house, so if you don't get us there, try Mike's."

"Why don't you and JM just stay in the cabin all year?"

"It's so much easier for JM to catch the bus at the house. When we're at the cabin one of us has to drive him to school every day."

Walking away, Sam said, "That makes sense. I'll let you know what I find out."

Chapter 26

Bill Dean Acts

For weeks the death of the Senator was front-page news. Every day Legs would scan the paper to see if Bill Dean had followed up on her story. She was getting so frustrated about not finding anything that she decided it was time to make another call. She changed her mind the next day when she found what she was looking for on the front page.

Is the GBI covering up a serial killer in Georgia?

The article went on to explain that an anonymous source had predicted the killing of the Senator and Judge. The source had also provided information that the killer, who was extremely skilled at covering his trail, had been on a spree for 15 years. Many of the cases had been closed as murder/suicides. It further stated the GBI had appointed a special task force to follow up and investigate the murders.

As she laid the paper on the table a smile came across her face. *Everything has fallen into place.*

Later as Legs drove to Charlie's she was on cloud nine. Dean had finally done his job of getting the GBI on the trail of the serial killer. She and Charlie no longer had to worry about being suspects. She turned the radio to her favorite station that only played 50s and 60s music. When her favorite song, "I only have eyes for you," began to play she knew her destiny was coming soon.

Now that the messy part of her plan was over she could concentrate on the wonderful life she had always wanted. When Charlie was appointed to fill the now vacant Senate seat, they could announce their engagement. She decided the wedding should take place just before the election. With Charlie being an incumbent and a newlywed he should win by a landslide. She thought, *What does the A Team leader on TV always say? Oh yeah, I love it when a plan comes together.*

As she drove up she could see that the front door was open and Charlie was sitting in the swing. She stopped singing along with the radio and yelled out the window, "Charlie Webb. You're getting lucky tonight." She had a skip in her step as she hit the front porch.

Charlie held up a glass filled with his favorite drink – vodka. "I'm glad you're happy. My day has turned to hell in a hand basket."

"What could be so bad? Our plan worked perfectly. That newspaper reporter has them looking for a serial killer, not us."

"Ah, that's not it. Would you believe Auntie thinks because she has a degree in political science and helped my uncle make some political decisions that she is qualified to fill his empty seat?"

The news made Legs go weak in the knees. In fact, she had to sit down. "Can she do that?"

"It seems this is the thing to do nowadays. Apparently three other wives did it in the last five years. Two of them were elected to the permanent seats."

"Let's not panic. We didn't come this far to just give up."

He looked up over his glass and said, "We could shoot her too."

"That's not the answer. There's no way we could make it look like a serial killer did it. But if she died in an accident, that's another story. There's one thing for certain; drinking is not the solution. Pour that drink out and I'll take you out to eat.

Chapter 27

Suspect List

The Barkley household was just sitting down to dinner when a car drove up the driveway. Jim answered the door and called back to the others, "It's Sam. He doesn't want anything to eat. Just to talk. We'll be on the front porch."

"What did you find out, Sam?"

"Not much. They have Walter in charge of the task force. Because it's an ongoing investigation, he can't discuss anything with me. He did let me know you're on the list of suspects and that he needed to question you."

"Did he say when?"

"No, but I'm sure he'll see you as soon as next week."

"That's okay with me. You know I had nothing to do with those deaths, don't you, Sam?"

"It never entered my mind."

At one time Sam had thought Jim might have been a serial killer, but after working so close to him for the past couple of years he knew Jim was too gentle to kill anything, much less a man.

Pacing, Jim said, "I'll feel better when I'm off the list."

Shaking his head with regret, Sam said, "I'm sorry. That's all I've got."

"I understand. You did all you could." Walking towards the kitchen Jim turned, "Are you sure you don't want to eat?"

"No thanks. I need to get home to Jane and the kids. I'll see you Monday."

Jim was surprised to see Walter Rogers and a state patrolman in front of Shirley's desk when he arrived at work on Monday, and commented, "You guys are fast."

Walter asked, "You were expecting us?"

"Yeah, Sam said you might be here."

"That's right; I did see him last week. I think he was disappointed when I couldn't tell him anything."

"He was, a little. But he understands. Can I offer you guys coffee?"

"No, this isn't a social call. I need to ask you some questions."

Turning to Shirley, he asked her to hold all his calls and directed the men back to his office.

Realizing he hadn't introduced the patrolman with him. Walter said, "Jim, this is Patrolman Mark Word. He and Sam worked together in the past."

"Nice to meet you. Sam should show up shortly and I'm sure he'll be glad to see you."

"That'll be nice."

"Now, what questions do you have?" asked Jim.

"First question. Where were you on the third Sunday of September?"

"That's easy, I was eating a picnic lunch with Dr. Amanda Hicks on the big island on Lake Blue Ridge."

"You answered that awfully fast," replied Walter.

"I guess so. I'm a lawyer. It was a logical guess."

"How can I get in touch with her?"

"She works at Fannin Regional."

"Did anyone else see you and the doctor fishing?"

"I guess the Barkleys and JM, my son."

"When was the last time you were in Dalton?" asked Walter.

"I've never been into Dalton. I don't think I've ever been west of Ellijay, in fact."

"Can you prove that?"

"Walter, how do you prove you've never been someplace?"

"Sorry, Jim. I guess you're right. Do you have any guns?"

"No, I don't have any. I've started trying to bow hunt."

"No guns of any kind? How about the Barkleys?" Walter asked.

"I really don't know."

"I think we have all we need from you right now."

As they walked out of the office, Sam came in.

"Hi there, Walter. What are you doing up in the mountains? And look at the company you're keeping." Grabbing Mark's hand he said, "It's really nice to see you."

"You, too," answered Mark.

"I guess this is an all business meeting, huh, Walter? How long will you be in town?"

"We've got to leave tonight. I have a meeting with the Governor tomorrow."

"The Governor? Aren't you special."

"Knock it off, Sam. I can still kick your butt," smiled Walter.

"Next time you're up, you've got to let Jane cook for you."

"I'll do that. Can you tell me the quickest way to the Sheriff's office?"

"Take that road across the railroad tracks, make a right, then the first left and you're there."

"Thanks."

"See you next time," said Sam.

Arriving at the Sheriff's office, Walter checked his watch and said to Mark, "We're a little pressed for time. Let me do all the talking."

"That's okay with me."

The Sheriff welcomed them into his office. He and Walter had become friends while Walter was trying to get Peggy released.

"I'd like to ask you a couple of quick questions about Clay Cagle's death."

"You're working this case?" the sheriff asked.

"Yeah. I'm heading the task force."

"Leave it to Cagle to get killed with someone important. What do you need from me?"

"First, can you tell me what cases he was working on and if anyone would benefit from his death?"

"I fired him a couple of months ago for planting evidence. I heard he was trying to be a private eye in Jasper," answered the sheriff.

"Did he have any involvement with Jim Coleman?"

"Funny you should ask. The reason I let him go involved the Coleman case."

After making that entry into his notes, Walter asked, "Was there anything else?"

"Yeah, Cagle was trying to build a child abuse case against Coleman. Coleman and Nick came to see me about Cagle falsifying evidence and requested I stop him from pursuing the child abuse charge. They made a big thing about Judge Foster and Cagle trying to frame him."

Walter's interest peaked and he asked, "Is that why you fired him?"

The sheriff answered, "Yes, I found all the proof I needed in his patrol car."

Getting ready to write in his notebook, Walter asked, "Do you think Coleman is capable of revenge?"

Sitting back in his chair, the sheriff thought for a minute, "Not really."

"Here's my card." He wrote his private number on the back and requested the Sheriff give him a call if he thought of anything else that might be relevant.

Chapter 28

Senator's Secretary

As Sam came into the office Friday, Jim asked, "Where have you been all week?"

"Investigating and spending some of your money. I don't think you'll like what I found."

Jim said "Let's go outside to talk." As they reached the parking lot, he asked Sam, "Okay, give me what you've got."

"I went to see Webb's secretary. She remembered you and how upset the Senator had been when you refused to take his son's case. I don't think she liked Webb too much."

"Why do you think that?"

"Because she couldn't wait to tell me everything she knew. The day the Senator received the package from you turning down his son's case she said he just lost it. He had her call a PI named Bill Long."

"Did you talk to him?" asked Jim.

"I did. That's where I spent your money. With the Senator dead, Long's loyalty was also dead. Greed is his motivator."

"Leave it to you to find his 'hot button'. How much did it take?"

"Five hundred."

"I was expecting a lot more. Was it worth it?"

"I think it was. The Senator directed Long to find any dirt he could on you and the judge handling his case. Long was really pissed 'cause when the charges were dropped Webb refused to pay him for his work."

"What about me?" asked Jim.

"That's the best part. When Long was here in Blue Ridge he found Judge Foster and introduced him to the Senator. Foster convinced Webb that taking JM from you would be the best revenge he could ever get."

"That's not the best part, Sam. It's the worst part. It ties me to all three murders. I can't believe anyone would hold that kind of grudge against me over a simple business decision. What else did Long do for them?"

"That's about it. When Foster came onboard, Long's services were no longer needed."

"You're right; I don't like what you found. Do you have any more good news?"

"Only that the secretary and Long both gave this info to Walter last week. It looks like you are not only on the list of suspects; you may be the whole list. "

"This is scary. When Peggy was on death row, I couldn't convince anyone I was the killer. Now when I'm innocent, all the evidence points to me. Sam, can you think of anyone who might want to frame me for some reason? Other than Walter, who knows the facts about Peggy and me? Do you think it's just coincidental or could someone really be trying to frame me?"

"I don't really think so. First, who could possibly know? And what would they get from doing it?"

"Okay, let's go with this. If someone knows about the other murders, then it stands to reason that what they are trying to accomplish is to kill one of those three for their own reasons while trying to make it look like I did it. Surely, Walter wouldn't think a child abuse case would be enough motivation to kill three people. I think the real issue is which one of those three they really wanted dead; maybe the other two were collateral damage."

"That would make sense. Let me try to find someone who would benefit from any of their deaths," suggested Sam.

"Sam, I'm worried. I don't like where this case is going and if we don't find something soon, the people in the Capital will want a sacrifice. When you think about me doing everything I could to convince Walter that I was the serial killer, not Peggy, this event could be the one thing that will get him off the fence about me. It looks and feels like someone is trying to make this a copy-cat killing, but what I don't understand is only three or four of us know enough to do that. Who else could possibly know?"

"Jim, is it possible that Peggy has kin that we don't know about?"

"I don't think so, but it's obvious somebody knows. Can you talk to Walter off the record to try to find out who might be doing this?"

"I'll try, but from what he's told me you're still his prime suspect."

Chapter 29

Alibi

Walter and Patrolman Word walked up to the receptionist desk at Fannin Regional. Seeing her nametag, Walter said, "Nancy, I'm Investigator Rogers." He showed her his badge and asked if they could see Dr. Hicks to ask her a few questions. Her smile disappeared with his request. The last two times she had interrupted Amanda with requests for her time to see investigators, she had gotten nasty. Dr. Amanda was known for shooting the messenger.

She hesitated at the doctor's door, gathered up her courage and knocked. Dr. Hicks looked up when Nancy's entered and when Nancy finished explaining what she wanted, Dr. Amanda said, "So they did come. Jim warned me they might. Show 'em in. It won't take long."

Walter made the introductions, "We know you're very busy, so I'll make this as quick as I can."

Smiling, Amanda said, "I appreciate that. How can I help?"

"Can you tell me where you were the third Sunday in September?"

She looked at her calendar, "That's easy. I was fishing with Jim Coleman."

"All day?"

"Most of the day. We left the dock at around 6 o'clock, fished all morning and then had a picnic lunch. I think we returned to the cabin about 2 or 3 in the afternoon."

Walter made an entry into his notes, "Anyone else see you there?"

"The Barkleys saw us leave in the morning and return in the afternoon."

"Good. Just a couple more questions and we'll be finished. Do you know anything about child abuse allegations against Mr. Coleman?"

The question caught her totally off guard. She stuttered and finally blurted out, "Yes, sir. A deputy sheriff asked me some questions this past summer."

"Do you remember his name?"

"No, but just a minute. He left me his card." Searching through her desk, she found it and she read out the name, "Deputy Clay Cagle."

As she looked up, she made the connection in her mind. "He's one of the men who was killed, isn't he?"

"Yes, ma'am he is. Do you remember what he asked?"

"Not really. Something about who was supervising JM when he had his accidents."

"How many accidents?"

"Really just two. He had a broken arm and he stepped on a nail a couple of months before that."

When he finished his entry into his notes, he asked, "Did he ask about anything else?"

"Not that I remember."

Standing up and signaling to Word that the meeting was over, Walter said, "Thanks, we'll get out of your hair now."

As soon as they left the hospital, Mandy called Jim.

"Jim, the GBI guy was here. He asked about that Sunday like you said he would."

"Was he satisfied with your answer?"

"He seemed to be, but then he asked me about the child abuse thing. Did you know that Cagle was the one who was killed with the Senator?"

"Yeah, I did. Don't worry about it. This is a high profile case and they don't have many leads. The reason they are interested in me is that I have a personal connection with two of the men killed and a business connection with the third. I'm worried that they may be trying to use this child abuse case to tie me to the killings."

"What do you mean by 'personal'?"

"Judge Foster is JM's uncle. He's always wanted to be in control of his estate. The feud about this has been going on since before Peggy's death. I think he was using Cagle to trump up bogus charges against me to justify taking me to court. You know I'd never abuse JM."

"Why would Cagle help Foster in the first place?"

"He was an ambitious little man. He wanted to be the sheriff in the worst way. For a couple of years I know of, maybe even longer, he's been planting evidence so he could get quick convictions. He had earned a reputation as a deputy that got things done. When Sam came to work for me, he quickly destroyed Clay's little playhouse. In less than six months Sam had found evidence we used to have three of the cases thrown out of court and cleared the last one. He even threatened Sam by saying he'd regret meddling in his business. I think his plan was to get me out of the picture and that would put Sam out of a job."

"How do you know the Senator?" she asked.

"He asked me to defend his son in a juvenile case and I turned him down. We only had two meetings. What exactly did you tell Walter?"

"I told him about the broken arm and the nail. I didn't tell him about Cagle asking me about your temper. Do you think I did something wrong?"

"I think you did just fine. You told the truth and he didn't ask. Why don't you come over and eat with the family tonight when you get off?"

"Wild horses couldn't keep me away. I need a big hug."

Chapter 30

New Suspect

As Walter drove into Jim's parking lot, he saw Sam coming out with two young boys. He quickly exited the car to catch him before he could get away.

"Sam, you're just who I'm looking for. Have you got a minute for me?"

"Yeah, a couple. The boys and I have an appointment to get a haircut. Boys, this is Walter Rogers. He's a GBI agent. Walter, this is Doug Crawford and Johnny McGill."

It was apparent the boys were impressed that Sam actually knew an agent. They timidly shook hands and then Sam asked them to wait in the car while he spoke with Walter.

Walter asked, "What's their story?"

"Johnny is the son of a friend, Sue McGill. They got in a little trouble and Jim defended them as a favor."

"That explains Jim's involvement, but what about yours?"

Red-faced, Sam answered, "Maybe I took responsibility for Doug."

Walter laughed and said, "I swear, I don't know which of you two has the biggest heart. Well, could you meet me later to answer some questions?"

"Sure, anything for you. Could I meet you at the Tastee Freeze for lunch?"

"That'd be great. I am getting hungry."

As they settled into a booth and completed their order, Sam asked, "What's on your mind?"

"Let's start with some basics. Where were you on the third Sunday of September?"

"Does this mean I'm a suspect?"

"Just answer the question. This is hard enough as it is."

"Let me think." Thumbing through his notes he said, "Oh, yeah. I was squirrel hunting."

"Was anyone with you?"

"Yep."

"Sam, stop that. Stop answering with just the basics. You're acting like a suspect. Just tell me what you did that day."

"Sorry, Walter. I've never been on this side before. Here's your answer. Mike and I took Michael and JM squirrel hunting most of the day."

"Why didn't Jim go?"

"He and Mandy went fishing." He held up both hands like quotation marks when he said fishing.

"Does that mean they didn't actually go fishing?"

"Oh, when they go fishing they never bring home any fish."

Concerned, Walter asked Sam, "Is that normal?"

"Yeah. I guess. According to them they release them after they're caught. Now, Walter, I ask you, what kind of fishing is that?"

"Back to the boys and squirrel hunting. Did you get any?"

"I got two, Mike got three and even Michael got one."

"How about JM?"

Smiling and shaking his head, Sam said, "Remember, JM is only 11."

Not understanding, Walter asked, "What's that got to do with it?"

"To be a good squirrel hunter you must sit perfectly still for a long period of time. Squirrel hunting is a lesson in patience. JM hasn't learned that lesson yet."

"What kind of guns did you guys use?"

"Mike and I had 20 gauges; the boys were using their 410s we gave them last summer for their birthdays."

Closing his notebook, Walter said, "I thought you used a .22 to kill squirrels."

"I did, but with this bummed up shoulder I'm not steady enough anymore."

"How about Mike?"

"He's worse than I am. He missed two with that shotgun. Walter, are you thinking Mike or I could have shot the Senator?"

"Relax, Sam. You know I have to close all the loose ends. Next and last question; Do you know anyone who could have made the shot that killed the Judge and the Senator?"

He laughed, "Half the men in Fannin County. They all hunt and have done so since they were boys. I think you better find another lead."

"I guess you're right."

"Questions over?"

"Yeah, why?"

"I need to talk to you as a friend, off the record."

"What have you got?"

"When Jim and I saw that editorial about the GBI covering up a serial killer we were wondering who the source was. Are you the source?"

"Sam, I'm surprised you'd even ask. You know I'm more professional than that."

"We thought so, but only a few people know some of the details that were given to this Dean fellow."

"I know. He was the first person I talked with. Dean told me he couldn't reveal his source; however, off the record he said he didn't know who she was. She'd only called him twice. The second time she was pissed that he hadn't exposed the threat and then she told him something big was going to happen."

"The Senator's death?" asked Sam.

"I assume that's what she was talking about."

"Walter, it sounds like she's your killer. Why are you spending so much time on Jim? If we hadn't worked on Peggy's defense would you still be checking him out?"

"I would like to think I would. I've just been following the evidence, and right now everything we've turned up points to Jim. Show me another direction and I'll follow it."

"Jim and I were thinking perhaps you should be looking at who would benefit from any of their deaths. We're thinking one of them was the real target and the other two were just collateral damage. Because everything points to Jim, this person must have access to classified information. I think if you find the answers to those two questions, you will find your killer."

"It makes sense and it really comes down to the Judge and Senator. Based on the evidence, Cagle was just in the wrong place at the wrong time."

"What makes you think that?"

"The sniper only shot twice, and Cagle had fired all but one bullet from his pistol. It looks like the sniper's first shot must have taken out the Judge and the Senator."

"Walter, if you don't mind, Jim has me digging too. We failed him on Peggy; I don't want to let him down again. I don't want to compromise your position, but I just want you to know I'll be trying to help."

"I welcome the help."

Chapter 31

Change In Plans

Legs drove straight from work on Friday to see Charlie. She had a plan and she knew if she didn't let him know soon he'd screw everything up. She was in his kitchen when he came home. He smelled of booze and obviously had not taken a bath for a week.

"Charlie, you look terrible. When's the last time you showered?"

He responded as if in a stupor, "Monday, I think."

She turned on the shower, "Take off your clothes and get in."

"I don't want one," he snapped.

"Well, you're getting one. You stink. Besides I need you clean and sober. I have a plan on how we can make you a Senator in about six to eight months."

When he heard those words, he perked up. "Really?"

"Absolutely. Now relax and let me rub the dirt away."

After the shower she fixed coffee and as they sat at the kitchen table she began to lay out the plan.

"Charlie, you're going to support your aunt's idea of her taking over his seat. In fact, for the next eight months you're going to be her right-hand man."

He could see where she was going with this plan. By being her special assistant he would be highly visible at the Capital building.

Legs continued, "If you work it right, everyone will think you're the real power behind all her decisions. Then if she were killed in a car accident, who would be a sure bet to replace her?"

As he thought through what she had proposed, he began to shed his defeated posture and resume the look of a successful lawyer.

"Legs, you're amazing. What a wonderful plan. It's even better than replacing my uncle. It will give me a trial period as Senator. If I mess up or miss something, they'll just blame her. On the other hand, if we do something great everyone will think it was me. Legs, you're wonderful. Will you marry me?"

"Yes, but not until you're a Senator. We've gone over this before."

"Do your kids know we're going to get married?"

"No, not yet. They may suspect it, but don't you dare tell them. We have a lot to do in the next few months and I don't want my kids in the way."

"Okay, okay."

"Charlie, in the next month or so I need for you to drive the back roads in the county and find an old car or truck you can buy. The more banged up the better. Something we can push over a cliff."

"Is that what we're going to use to stage my aunt's car accident?" he asked.

"Exactly."

Chapter 32

Jim's Frustration

Jim couldn't just stand around waiting to hear Sam's updates. As luck would have it his case load was slow and he had nothing to do. He was bored. His calendar was empty by design, as he had been sworn in as a Judge last month. This waiting was slowly driving him insane. He walked to Shirley's desk and asked, "Would you get Nancy on the phone for me, please?"

Shirley was pleased to be able to do anything for him, as lately all she had done was worry. She was looking forward to the increase in work that would come with his new position. After quickly doing as he requested, she called out, "Nancy is on Line 1."

"Nancy, this is Jim. Is there any way I could talk with Mandy?"

"You're in luck. She's in her office eating a sandwich."

Mandy came on the line. "Sweetie, it's so nice to hear your voice. How did I earn this wonderful surprise?"

"I was just missing you and figured we could plan a fishing trip this weekend. Just you and me, all day."

"James T. Coleman, are you kidding me?"

"What do you mean? What does the T stand for?"

"T stands for trouble – big trouble. You know Mother and I are going to Lenox Square this weekend to find my wedding dress!"

"Oh my God! I forgot all about it."

"Did you also forget we're getting married on Thanksgiving?"

"No, sweetie. I can't wait. I just got caught up with this GBI investigation and lost my focus."

"Why don't you pick up a pizza and meet me at the apartment around 6:30? When you leave tonight I bet you'll have your focus back."

Chapter 33

Another Call

Weeks had passed with nothing in the paper on the Senator's death. At first they talked like the GBI had an obvious suspect. After not seeing any follow-up articles, Legs began to worry. She didn't say anything to Charlie as he would just panic, and that wasn't what they needed now. She decided to make one final call to Bill Dean. If done right, she could send the investigators on a false trail.

The next day during lunch she made her way to an isolated phone booth and dialed the *Journal*. This time when Dean answered she heard something strange. As a young girl, her parents had a party line and she easily recognized the sound made when someone else was on the line. Startled, she said, "Mr. Dean?"

Fear flooded through her and she slammed down the phone. For the first time in her life she realized she could go to jail. With the fear came nausea. She walked quickly to the ladies room. Three steps from the door, she could no longer hold it. Just returning from lunch, several of her co-workers, walked up just as she vomited in the hall. They all ran to her side to help.

Concerned, one of them said, "You need to go home. We'll cover for you."

Getting some of her composure back, she quickly accepted their offer. Once in the parking lot she just sat in her car thinking, *He was tracing my call.* She was still weak in the knees as she drove away. She drove aimlessly until she saw the Canton 18 miles sign. That's when it hit her. *I can call from there. So what? Let them trace the call.* Now she had a new strategy and the closer she got to her destination the more she relaxed.

As she drove by the old cotton mill, she saw a McDonalds. Across the street was a service station with a phone booth. She pulled up to it before she realized she didn't have any change. She ran across the street to McDonalds to fix that problem. Ordering a hamburger, Coke and fries to go, she handed the cashier a ten-dollar bill and requested all coins for her change, telling the attendant she needed to make a long distance call. Gathering the change she walked to the car and placed the Coke and bag on the front seat. She removed the napkins from the bag to hold the phone while she made the call. An operator said, "Deposit fifty cents for the first three minutes."

She thought that's all she'd need. When Dean answered, she said, "It's me. How's your investigation going?"

Again she heard the sound of another receiver being picked up.

"Not well. I think they're running out of leads. Can you help us?"

"I've told you everything I know. He's right there in front of you. The reason I called is I think he has killed again because he plans on leaving the state before Christmas, maybe even Thanksgiving."

"That's only a month away."

"I know. I also know he always kills someone before he leaves and then stays in his new location until his money runs out. So that tells me he's either already killed or plans to shortly."

"Are you going?" asked Dean.

"No way. He wants me to keep my job so he'll have a place to come back to."

"Will he come back?"

"He always does. Here he comes. Bye." She hung up.

Quickly, she wiped off all areas she might have touched. Getting into her car she drove slowly out of the parking lot back towards home. After driving from the station she met a patrol car going the opposite direction with red lights running. After another 500 yards she met a patrol car coming out of a side road. In less than two miles she had seen 4 police cars heading towards McDonalds. About five miles later she realized she was home free which gave her a major adrenaline rush. She had done it. She'd gotten away with it. The rush was so intense, she thought, *If only Charlie could make me feel this good.*

Chapter 34

The Set Up

Addressing the officer sitting at the next desk, Bill Dean asked, "Did they get her?"

"No. There wasn't anyone at the phone booth. The state patrol is checking the area for witnesses now."

Worried he'd be cut out of the loop, Dean said, "I expect you to keep me informed on what you find. That was our agreement when I let you tap my phone."

"Mr. Rogers filled me in on that and I'm giving you everything as I get it."

"My reputation is on the line. This is the first time I've ever given up a source. If it gets out, I'll never live it down."

"I understand. I'm sure you made the right decision."

In about three hours the office received a phone call giving them an update.

"Mr. Dean, they think they have a witness -- a cashier at the McDonalds across from the phone booth. He described her as an older woman with blond hair. Apparently she was well built, as he said she looked sexy for an old woman. She paid him with a ten-dollar bill and asked for change to use the phone. The investigating officer has the ten-dollar bill and is checking it for prints."

"Can you get prints off of money?" asked Dean.

"Yeah, but the problem is there are usually too many of them. Mr. Rogers doesn't think she'll call again, so I'm removing the tap on your phone."

Again concerned, Dean asked. "That doesn't mean I'm out of the loop, does it?"

"I don't think so. Agent Rogers seems to be a man of his word."

"I hope so," said Dean.

Chapter 35

Dalton Sheriff

Walter asked Mark, "Did you find any usable prints on the money?"

"They found three different ones. One was the cashier and the other two were for unknown subjects at this time."

Shaking his head in frustration, Walter said, "Damn it, another dead end. Let's drive over to Dalton and do some checking on that Gibson case. The informant seems to put a lot of stock in the fact they were murdered."

"I agree. We need to get a break on this case. How can three people be killed without any trace of the killer?"

"That does indicate the murders were well planned. That's the trait of a serial killer," noted Walter.

After a quick run up I-75, Rogers and Word walked into Sheriff Ken Dixon's office. He seemed a little miffed about all the attention he was getting about the death of the Gibsons. His ego was bruised that anyone would second guess any of his cases. He'd been Sheriff for 14 years and with his experience he felt no one should ever question his competency.

Trying to cover his true feelings he welcomed them into his office. "Come on in and take a seat. I can't believe you're still checking the Gibson case. Like I told the other investigators it was a very simple case. There were only two victims with no sign of forced entry. The gun was still in old Ben's hands."

"From the notes I see that you thought there was a third person in the house," Walter said. "Was that person ever located?"

"No. I didn't even look. It was obvious to me that Ray was having sex with another underage girl and old Ben just snapped. I didn't want to embarrass the girl or her family."

"Do you have any idea who she was?" Walter asked.

"Not really. It would have been a waste of time and effort," answered the Sheriff.

"Could we see the evidence on the case?" Mark asked.

"Sure." He called one of his deputies and instructed him to retrieve it.

Agent Rogers was surprised to see him return with a container half the size of a shoebox. "Is that it? Where's the rifle?"

"That's it. I returned the rifle to Mrs. Gibson." Sarcastically he added, "It was her property."

Rogers opened the box to find a pair of cotton panties, one complete 30-06 round, one empty shell and a small plastic bag containing two spent bullets. Looking at the Sheriff he asked, "Where is the other empty shell?"

Surprised at the question, he said, "Isn't it there?"

"No, I don't even see one listed on the inventory sheet."

Coming out of his chair, Sheriff Dixon said, "Let me see that. I'll be damned. I would have sworn it was there."

"Are your people in the habit of losing evidence?" asked Rogers with a little sarcasm of his own.

Embarrassed, the Sheriff called in the two deputies who had been on the investigation with him. When questioned about the missing shell, they both confirmed they'd never seen the second one. One deputy added he had removed one empty shell from the rifle and dusted it for prints. He was disappointed that he could only get a partial print. Rogers asked, "Whose print was it?"

The deputy answered, "I don't know. We couldn't find a match."

A little upset, Rogers asked, "Did anyone see a second shell?"

All three looked at each other.

The first deputy said, "I didn't."

"Neither did I," replied the second deputy.

The red-faced Sheriff summed it up, "I guess we all overlooked it."

Rogers answered, "I guess so. We could go see Mrs. Gibson and see if we can find it."

Hesitantly the Sheriff asked, "Do we need to do that? It's been almost a year since it happened. I would hate to upset her."

"Don't you think it would make her feel better if she knew her husband didn't kill her son?"

"Are you saying they were both murdered?"

"I'm beginning to believe that's exactly what happened. Before you returned the rifle did you make sure both bullets were fired from the same gun?"

Agent Rogers was asking some very embarrassing questions. In his haste to make sure Mrs. Gibson and the unknown minor were not harassed, he had taken short cuts that might have destroyed this case. His cockiness and superior attitude may have just destroyed his well-earned reputation as a professional. Looking at Rogers with real concern in his eyes he asked, "How can we fix this screw up?"

Seeing that the Sheriff was sincere in his question, Rogers answered, "I think we need to reopen the case and see where the evidence takes us."

Relieved that Rogers hadn't removed him from the case, the Sheriff offered, "My entire department is at your disposal. Just tell us what to do."

"First, we need to see Mrs. Gibson and get that rifle back. Also we need to find out from her if anything unusual happened in the months prior to their deaths."

Seeing that he might save some face after all, he answered, "If you don't mind, I'll drive the two of you out there right now."

"I think that would be the best way to approach it. She knows you and right now we only have a hunch."

They quickly drove the few miles to the Gibson house.

The housekeeper met them at the door. "Sheriff, Mrs. Gibson is out at the club playing bridge. She'll be gone until nine tonight. I'll be leaving at five. Do you want me to call her?"

"No, I should have called before I came over. I'll make an appointment next time. By the way, Mrs. Waters, you don't happen to know where she put that old Army rifle I returned to her last summer, do you?"

"Sure do. It's in the closet next to the front door."

"Could you get it for me? We'd like to check it one more time."

"I guess Mrs. Gibson wouldn't mind. She doesn't like guns anyway; especially that one."

As they drove back to the Sheriff's office he agreed that Rogers should take the rifle and bullets and do all the ballistic testing at GBI headquarters. When parting, Rogers could see the Sheriff's attitude and demeanor had changed drastically since the time of their arrival. He commented to Mark on the way back to Atlanta, "The Sheriff screwed the pooch on this one and he knows it."

"Do you think we can salvage it?"

"I hope so. Solving his case may help solve ours."

Chapter 36

New Leads

"Mark, we got the results back on the bullets from the Gibson case. Would you believe they were fired from two different rifles? The bullet that killed the son came from the same rifle that killed the Senator."

"That really opens a can of worms," Mark said.

"You're right, and there's even more. The partial print on the casing matches one of the prints on our $10 bill," explained Rogers.

Coming to a decision, Mark said, "So it looks like our informant is really the killer."

"Or an accomplice. Two rifles were used at the Gibson house. Why would she use two rifles if she was the only one there?" Rogers asked.

"That makes sense. They're not as smart as we thought. I guess they didn't expect the county sheriff to check the ballistics."

Walking towards the door Rogers said, "And he didn't. I wonder what else they screwed up. Let's go see the Sheriff."

When they arrived at Dixon's office he seemed truly glad to see them. "Agent Rogers, please come in. I have some good news."

"Please call me Walter. I have good news, too. You go first."

"I talked with Mrs. Gibson. She found that just a week before Ben's death he had taken all the cash out of his safety deposit box, savings and checking accounts. She said it had to be almost $200,000."

Pulling out his notebook, Walter asked, "Does she know where it went?"

"No. But, she thinks it had something to do with Ray. A short time before the shooting old Ben had given Ray an ultimatum – get a job or get out."

"That gives us another piece of the puzzle. The bullets you gave us came from two rifles. The rifle that killed Ray was also the rifle used in the Senator's case. Mark and I feel because two rifles were used there had to be at least two killers involved."

"So you're saying old Ben was murdered?"

"The evidence points in that direction. Also the partial print your deputy lifted matches one we have on file for an informant."

"What's the informant's name?" asked Dixon.

"We don't know. All we have is her description. She's a tall, athletic blond. Does that description mean anything to you?"

"Not to me, but it could to one of my deputies."

Walter handed the Sheriff a photo of Jim and asked if he or any of his deputies had ever seen him in Dalton.

"I haven't, but I'll check with the guys."

"Sheriff, I need for you to keep everything we've discussed to yourself. I don't want the killers to know what we know about them. They've made a mistake or two and we want them to make a few more. Right now silence about the case is our best approach."

"What about telling Mrs. Gibson?"

"Absolutely not. Better news would be that we had the killers in jail." suggested Walter.

"Makes sense. We'll stay quiet as a mouse until you tell us otherwise."

Walter headed for the door and said, "Thanks, I'll keep you informed."

Walter had a gnawing feeling in his stomach. His suspicions kept coming back to the same person, Jim Coleman. He knew he had to eliminate these feelings before he was ever going to be able to think outside the box. He made a couple of calls and then developed a plan on how he would clear this from his mind once and for all.

On Tuesday, he decided to drive to Jim's office. Stopping for breakfast he arrived a little after ten in the morning. When he walked in Shirley recognized him immediately. "Mr. Rogers, Jim's in court today."

"Oh, I'm sorry. I should have called first."

"He should be back around five this evening. He always checks in before he goes home. Is it important?"

"No, this is just a social visit. I was in town and thought I'd just drop by."

"He'll be sorry he missed you."

"Speaking of a social life, has Jim gotten serious about that girl yet?"

"Oh yeah. He's in 'luv'. He acts like a kid around her."

Casually, Walter bluffed with, "That's great. Is she that tall blond I met before?"

"Oh there've been four or five since then. It seems like every time he defends a teenager who has a single mom she immediately decides he should be her kid's father figure. After he turns them down two or three times they just seem to go away. The exception was that blond you're asking about – well, not really blond but dishwater blond. She perceived his rejection as him playing hard to get. She finally gave up when she found out he was in love with a doctor. And is he in love."

"Is this one a blond too?"

"Hardly, she's a petite brunette."

"Well then, who was the blond?"

"Ah, that was Irene Johnson. You know, I think she works for you at GBI headquarters. When she called the last time I'd never heard a woman that mad before. She made a lot of nasty threats."

"What did Jim do about that?"

"Nothing. You know Jim. He just said she'll get over it and I guess she did."

"Guess so. I'm glad he found someone. Tell him I'll see him next time I'm up here."

He returned to Atlanta with this new information.

Chapter 37

Irene Johnson

Walking into Walter's office Mark asked, "How did your visit to Blue Ridge work out?"

"I thought I was onto something when Shirley Wilson gave me the name of Irene Johnson. She's a tall blond that Jim dated awhile back."

"You think she's trying to screw Coleman because he dumped her?"

"Something like that."

"What did you find out?"

"Well, believe it or not, she works right here in the building. I went to personnel and got her file. Here's her picture and I checked her prints against the one on the money – no match."

"Looks like it turned out to be just another false lead."

"Maybe, but before I dropped it I thought we could show her picture to the cashier in Canton."

It took a little more than an hour to get there, but the person they needed to see had not reported to work. As they waited Mark asked Walter why he was so determined to find something on Jim Coleman. Walter was surprised that Mark had that perception about his investigation of the case.

Lying, he answered, "I guess because we haven't found anyone else that would benefit from the Senator and Judge Foster's deaths."

"Oh, I thought you had some sort of grudge."

"No, I am getting a lot of pressure from the Governor to find the killer," answered Walter.

"Yeah, I bet. This is an election year."

"Politics can cause a man to do some foolish things."

The cashier came to their table saying, "I'm Jimmy Jones. Are you looking for me?"

"Are you the one that took the $10 bill from the lady?" asked Walter.

"Yes, sir, I am."

"Could you look at this picture and tell me if this is the woman?"

"No, sir. The woman who gave me the money was much prettier."

"Thanks, Jimmy. That's all we need."

On their way back to the office Mark said, "I guess that means we take Coleman off our list."

"Not yet. Not until we find someone better to replace him."

Mark laughed, "I heard you were stubborn."

"I guess they're right."

When they got back to the office his secretary jumped out of her chair saying, "There's a special meeting in the conference room and they want you there."

He quickly walked to the meeting while Mark waited in his office. About an hour later Walter returned. Mark asked, "What's up?"

"The Governor is placing a lot of pressure on my boss to bring in the FBI."

"How can he do that? The murders occurred in Georgia."

"They seem to think that because he was a state Senator they can bend the rules."

"How long do we have before they step in?"

"Possibly until the first of the year."

Mark asked, "Do you think you can hold him off for more than two months?"

"A man can hope."

"What's our next step?"

Talking Rock

"I want to interview the Senator's wife. I heard she will take over her husband's seat until the next election. If she is able to take on his job, maybe she can help us find the reason someone wanted him dead."

Mark asked, "When do we meet her?"

"I've already instructed Holle to call and set up an appointment as soon as she can after Thanksgiving."

Chapter 38

Wedding Dress

As Mandy stopped her car in front of the Barkley's house she could see Mother waiting patiently on the front porch. Mother opened the passenger side door before Mandy could get out of the car. She got settled and adjusted her seatbelt before asking, "Mandy, are you excited?"

With a big grin, Mandy said, "I've dreamed of this day ever since I was a little girl. I was beginning to doubt if I'd ever get married, much less go looking for the perfect wedding dress."

Reaching over and placing her hand on Mandy's, Mother said, "And I'm so glad I get to share this with you."

"When I lost my mother as a little girl, I thought I'd also lost any possibility of sharing this day with someone so special. Thank you, Mother, for taking the time to shop with me."

"Child, I wouldn't miss this for the world! Would you believe Mike laughed at me all last night because I couldn't sleep?"

Recognizing an opportunity to get to know her better, Mandy asked, "How did you and Mike meet?"

"Oh, that's a long story."

"Well, we have two hours before we get to Lenox Square and the two hours back home. Can you tell your story in that time?"

"Sure, but you'd get bored."

"I'll take that chance. Who introduced you?"

"His younger brother, Jesse. When I was a girl, my father had a grist mill near Barnes Chapel Church. He dammed up a small stream they now call Stillhouse Creek. It runs into Sugar Creek about two miles before it empties into the Toccoa River. When I was a child there was a small school in the church house."

"Is it still there?"

"Yes, the church is still there. It's called New River Baptist now."

"I think I know where you're talking about. Isn't that called Galloway Road?"

"Galloway! That's what they called the school when I went there. It was a first through eighth grade school and then you went to Epworth for high school."

"Is that where you met Mike?"

"Lordy, no. I told you I met him at the grist mill. His brother, Jesse, used to bring a toe sack full of corn to be ground into cornmeal once a week. In fact, everybody from miles around would bring their corn to Daddy. He would grind it into meal for them."

"Mother, what in the world is a toe sack?"

Mother laughed and explained, "When we were kids, that's what we called a burlap bag."

"That's a lot of corn. I guess your father stayed pretty busy and made a lot of money."

"Well, he did stay busy, but no one had any money back then. Daddy would grind it for a share. When he finished he had a large can and a small one he used to measure out his share. He didn't make very much money. In fact, when he got a job working for the Tennessee Copper Company, he closed the grist mill down for keeps. I think the only thing that's left now is a part of the old dam."

"So, that's how you met Mike?"

"Do you want to hear the story, or not?"

"I'm sorry. No one ever said I was patient."

"At first, one of Jesse's chores was to bring the corn each week. I can still see him riding up on his mule now -- barefooted with overalls about 6 inches too short. One day he brought his brother, Mike, with him." She laughed then and continued, "You know I don't think I ever saw Jesse at the mill again!"

"Was it love at first sight?"

"I'm not sure about Mike, but it took a while for me."

"Did they go to the same school as you did?"

"Well, they were supposed to. I don't ever remember seeing Mike there, but I did see Jesse."

"You said it was a small school house. How could you not see them?"

"School was a lot different back then. It was a luxury to attend school, not a requirement. Life was hard on the farm. Boys were required to cut wood for the fireplace and wood stove. There were very few times during the fall or winter that boys got to attend every day. Girls came more often, and, as a result, we were way ahead of the boys when it came to education. Most boys dropped out completely before they became teenagers."

"Did Mike drop out?"

"Yes, in fact, well before he started high school."

"I don't understand. You need a high school education to be a postmaster."

"Yes, you do."

"How did he do it?"

"Mike and Jesse were both drafted during WW2. Mike and I married about two years before Pearl Harbor. In fact, he was just about to go to work for the company when he got his draft notice. While in the Army he was given the additional duty to be the mail clerk for his company. Mike loved the work and when the war was over, he used the GI Bill to get the education he needed. Because he was a veteran he was put on top of the hiring list. He started out as a mail carrier and the rest is history."

Laughing, Mandy said, "You make it sound like the war wasn't all that bad."

"It changed a lot of people's lives. In our case it changed our lives for the better. It even helped Mike to get over being so shy."

Realizing what Mother had said, Mandy asked, "Mike Barkley was shy? I can't believe that."

"Honestly, I don't think I've ever known a more bashful boy. He'd been coming every week for six months and all he could do was stand around and kick rocks. Would you believe he'd stay there for the couple of hours it took to grind his meal and never say one word to me?"

"Did you give him a chance?"

"Lord, yes. In fact, Mother would get so mad at me she couldn't even talk. I'd waste two hours hanging around hoping he'd talk to me. I can hear her now saying, 'Those chores aren't getting done while you're standing around making goo-goo eyes at that Barkley boy!' Then one day, I decided I couldn't stand it any longer. I saw him coming up the road. I waited for him at the corner of the grist mill and when he slid off the mule I surprised him by giving him a kiss right on the lips."

"What did he do?"

"He turned a bright red and tried to talk, but nothing would come out."

"What did you do?"

"What could a girl do? I ran back into the house. It worked, though. A month later he kissed me. You know when I say it out loud it sounds like it took a long time, but I remember it being a very fast courtship. But if I hadn't taken the first step, we'd still be courting, or sparking, as we called it back then."

"You know, Mike and Jim have a lot in common. How did he pop the question?"

Embarrassed, Mother whispered, "Don't you tell him I said this, but I asked him to marry me. For the life of me I can't even remember him saying yes, but we did get married. Mandy, he's the only man I've ever loved."

"Mother, Jim is the only man I've ever truly loved."

As they drove into the mall parking lot, Mother said, "Well, girl, let's go find that special dress for your wedding. We want you looking beautiful for my boys."

Five hours later they were on their way back to Blue Ridge. Mother said, "Your dress is beautiful. With your shoes and veil, you look like a princess."

"That's the way it makes me feel. I've always dreamed of finding the perfect wedding dress. I wasn't sure what it would look like. I just knew I'd know it when I put it on, and I did."

"Mandy, how old were you when your mother died?"

"I'd just turned eleven. It was just Dad and me after that and he spoiled me rotten. Until I met Jim he had ruined me for any other man. Even in high school the boys couldn't live up to the standard I had set for them."

Mother laughed. "I guess your baptism in Blue Ridge Lake changed all that."

"I didn't think so on that day, but you're right. It was a turning point in my life."

They both laughed as Mother said, "Aren't men wonderful?"

"Tell me about your wedding. What did you wear?"

"Oh, getting married back then wasn't as big an event as it is now days. I wore what we called our Sunday-go-to-meeting dress. I think it had blue flowers on it. In fact, I have a quilt I made with some of the fabric while I was pregnant with Michael."

"Would you show it to me?"

"Yes, just remind me when we get home. It's in the cedar chest at the foot of our bed."

"Where did you get married and how many people were there?"

"Mike, his older sister, Ruth, and I went to Reverend Corn's house over near Gravely Gap."

"Your parents weren't there?"

Laughing, Mother said, "I told you Mike was so afraid of my mother that he convinced me to wait and tell them afterwards."

"How'd they take it?"

Again, Mother laughed. "You could have knocked Mike over with a feather when Daddy said, 'It's about time.'"

"Was it a long ceremony?"

"Not really. It was over in fifteen minutes. I remember Mike offered the Reverend two dollars. That was almost a week's earnings. I'll never forget the expression on Mike's face when he told him, 'No, son. You don't have to pay me. You'll be paying for the rest of your life.' And to hear Mike tell it, he has."

Mandy said, "Mother, it sounds like a perfect wedding. I just hope Jim and I are half as happy as you two seem to be."

Chapter 39

Car Search

"Charlie, how's your search for an old car or truck coming along?"

"I found two, but they wanted too much money for them. I made an offer on a third one, but when I went back, would you believe they'd already sold it?"

"I can't believe you. Are you looking for a deal or a car you can use to kill your aunt?"

When he heard it said like that, he realized just how stupid it must have sounded to her. He had let himself get so caught up in the thrill of the search that he'd forgotten why he needed it in the first place. He and his father had spent many a Sunday afternoon looking for old trucks together and all those feelings had come flooding back. Those were the only good memories he had of his father. He knew for certain he didn't want Legs involved so he lied and said, "Don't worry. I've seen a couple more I plan to check out this weekend."

"Do you want me to go with you?"

"No, I can do it myself. It wouldn't look right if you were with me. They'd never believe I was looking for a car to restore."

"Is that the story you're telling?"

"Yes."

"I like it. Just remember you need to find one that's fast and big enough to push her off the road."

"Then I'll focus on getting an old pickup."

"Whatever, but we need it by February."

"Is that when it'll happen?"

"I was thinking February is the worst winter month we have and we should take advantage of that."

"That would be good. Annie visits her sister in Talking Rock twice a month. The road is narrow and curvy. If the weather is bad everyone will believe it was just an accident."

"You know, I've lived here all my life and never did know how Talking Rock got its name."

Charlie puffed up his chest and said, "There are a lot of legends. One says that the Indians had a boulder in Rock Creek with the inscription *Turn Me Over*. After they turned it over the other side said, *Now turn me back over so I can fool someone else*. The Cherokee Indians must have really had a sense of humor. They called it Nunya Gunwaniski, which means a rock that talks in Cherokee. The legend that I believe is that the rock bluff causes your voice to echo when you talk."

She said, "How'd you know that?"

"It was a school project when I was in high school.

"I'm impressed and I also like your plan. Now all we need is the truck."

"I'll find one this weekend."

Chapter 40

A Visit With The Senator

"Mark, Holle arranged an appointment for us with Senator Webb tomorrow morning at 10 a.m. in her office."

Dropping into Walter's easy chair, Mark said, "I thought they were in recess for the holidays."

"Congress is, but Holle says the Senator is just remodeling the office now. Meet me in the parking lot about 9:30 a.m. and we'll drive over together. Hey, why don't you take the rest of the day off with your family and I'll see you tomorrow?"

Mark was surprised to see Walter sitting in his car drinking coffee when he arrived at 9 a.m.

"How'd you know I'd be early?"

"You're an old military man. You guys think if you're on time you're 15 minutes late."

Smiling, Mark answered, "You're right. How'd you know that? You weren't in the military."

"Sam Wright was, and if he said it once he said it a thousand times. Get in, we might as well go."

Senator Webb had alerted her security guard that they were expected. He was a retired police officer and while en route to her office he filled the time with his own war stories. When the guard left, Mark commented, "It's been a long time since I've had such a friendly welcome on an official visit."

"You're right. I just hope the time with her goes as well."

Walter didn't know what he expected to see when he entered her office, but the sight of the secretary in a sweatshirt and blue jeans was a real surprise. Looking up from the box she was packing she said, "You must be Agent Rogers."

"Yes, ma'am, I am."

Coming around the box she said, "Follow me."

Walter and Mark obeyed. The sight of the Senator dressed as casually as her assistant raised both of their eyebrows. Catching the expression, the Senator said, "I'll bet you never expected to see me in blue jeans – especially since I'm a woman."

Smiling, Walter answered, "No, ma'am, but for some reason I feel better about our leadership now."

"Mr. Rogers, I'm supposed to be the politician, but your flattery is welcome."

All three of them looked up as a man dressed in a well-tailored suit entered the office carrying a box of pictures to be placed on the wall. She introduced him by saying, "Mr. Rogers, this is my assistant, Charlie."

Offering his hand, Walter said, "Nice to meet you, Charlie." Remembering his manners, he introduced Mark by saying, "Senator, Charlie, this is Investigator Mark Word."

They all shook hands and Walter asked if he could have a few moments alone with the Senator. She dismissed Charlie like a small child. The expression on his face revealed his true feelings; however, he did leave. Walter explained he understood that it would be devastating to discuss the death of her husband, but he needed her help to find the killer. She stated her appreciation for his concern but emphasized she was ready to help in any way she could. She asked that he be very candid in asking his questions. The first question Walter asked was the obvious one; "Do you know anyone who might want him dead?"

She answered, "I could probably give you a dozen names."

"Let's keep the list short. Who in the last twelve months would be on that list?"

Talking Rock

"Judge Edward in Cobb County, a lawyer named James Coleman and Principal Stockwell at Brent's high school."

Writing the names in his notebook, Walter asked, "Do you know why they would want revenge?"

"I'm not sure they would. These are just three names I heard my husband cursing in the last six months. He threatened to put them in their place."

"You don't have to answer this if you don't want to, but I need to ask. Your husband had a reputation of being someone you never wanted to cross. Can you explain if it's true, and if it is, why?"

"It is true. When my husband was first elected he was very ambitious, but he was also naïve to the ways of politics. Nearly ten years ago one of his fellow Senators persuaded him to support a bill he was introducing. In exchange that man promised to help my husband get a bill through that he'd been working on since he was elected. What Clark didn't know was the other guy was setting him up. He wanted to ruin Clark's reputation and credibility. The bill fell through and because of that Clark's bill couldn't even get out of committee. From that day forward my husband lost all compassion for anyone."

Still writing he asked, "Did he do anything?"

"I'll say. He spent over $200,000 hiring investigators to find something he could use against that other Senator."

Flipping the page of his notebook he asked, "Did they find anything?"

"A great deal. He came from a wealthy family and when young he had done lots of unsavory things that the family paid thousands of dollars to suppress."

"Did he do anything with the information?"

"About six months before the Senator's re-election, Clark gave all that information to a few reporters. He even paid some of them to make sure they reported it. With this information out, he lost the election. Clark even went to the extreme of making sure everyone knew that he was the one who had taken this guy down. He also let them know he had an investigator on retainer."

"Who is the private eye?"

Pulling a card from her desk and handing it to Walter she said, "Bill Long in Cartersville."

Without warning the door opened. Charlie came in with a tray of coffee and doughnuts. The Senator was a little surprised and embarrassed, but recovered quickly by asking if anyone was interested in the refreshments. Walter and Mark accepted the coffee and Mark munched on a doughnut while they continued to listen to the Senator's story. Charlie stood there like a butler waiting to be dismissed. It was obvious that he wanted to stay. With irritation in her voice, the Senator said, "That will be all, Charlie. Could you continue to help Lisa load the books?"

He stormed out of her office, still acting spoiled. When he was gone, she asked, "Do you have any other questions?"

"No, but if I think of anything, could I just call you?"

"That would be fine. I hope you find the killer soon."

"Wait, I do have one last question. I've been doing this for a long time, so please forgive me if I am wrong, but I am sensing that you were not close to your husband."

"No, your comment doesn't offend me. We were not close and hadn't been for years. We only stayed together for his career. I didn't love or hate him; I guess you could say I was just indifferent towards him. I know this opens another can of worms. Did a jealous husband do it? For my money, probably so."

"Senator Webb, thanks for your time and candor. Your office is looking nice."

Standing she shook his hand and said, "You're becoming quite the politician."

As Mark and Walter drove back to the office, Mark laughed and asked, "Who was that mousy little assistant?"

"Charlie?" asked Walter.

"Yeah. That's his name."

"That's her nephew."

"I've never seen such a brownnoser and suck up in all my life."

"Charlie is one of those people who thinks brownnosing is better than doing your job. They're the type who blame everyone when they fail to get promoted."

"Well, he's so mousy looking I don't think he's capable of doing any job well."

Chapter 41

Wedding Day

It was 6 a.m. and Mandy was wide awake. It had finally arrived, that special day – her wedding day. She and Mother had found the perfect wedding gown and she had tried it on at least ten times. Jane was supposed to arrive around 9 a.m. to help her get ready. As she laid her dress across the bed, she thought about the day ahead. She was somewhat disappointed, but pleased at the same time, that her old friends and distant cousins from Richmond had turned down her invitation to the wedding. She knew they didn't want to come to the sticks here in Blue Ridge, and all of them had used the excuse that she hadn't given them enough notice to make it happen. The real reason she was happy with their decision was that she wouldn't need to meet them at the Atlanta Airport on one of the busiest days of the year. It sounded selfish, but it was her day and she didn't want to start it by being a taxi driver.

At 8:30 a.m. Jane knocked on the door. Mandy almost ran to let her in, as she was so excited. She tried to sit quietly while Jane fixed her hair, but this led her to wonder what Jim was doing. Was he as nervous as she? She wasn't nervous about her decision to marry Jim, but she wanted everything to go smoothly.

Jim had woken before dawn and had cut himself three times while shaving. When Mike saw his wounds, he gave that big belly laugh of his, and said, "Jim-boy, this reminds me of when you first arrived here and tried to shave in that cold water at the gas station. You looked like you fell into a briar patch."

Jim nodded. "Yeah, I remember. That seems like a lifetime ago."

"It was. We've had some bad times, but mostly good ones since those days."

"I agree. Mike, thanks for lining up Reverend Harper to do our ceremony."

"I didn't do anything. I just greased the skids. In fact, I think he's honored that you asked him. He feels a kindred spirit to you because of how he married you and Peggy while she was in jail." They were both saddened with the memory of their failure to stop her execution for the murder of her father and brother.

"That was a rushed wedding ceremony. I hope he'll take his time today."

Mike laughed. "You may be sorry you said that. He can get pretty long-winded at times. What did he say to you when you asked?"

Jim smiled. "He said, 'You get her in front of me and I'll get you married.'"

Mike slapped his leg. "My God that sounds just like him!"

Mother walked in and said, "Would you two stop joking and drinking coffee. There's plenty to do. You're getting married at noon and we're eating Thanksgiving dinner at three. I need forty chairs set up for the guests and it looks like they're all staying for dinner."

When Jane and Mandy arrived at the Barkley's they went in through the back door. Mandy whispered to Mother, "Do you think I could talk to JM before the wedding? I have a gift for him."

"I don't see why not." She left the room, returned quickly with JM, and then left the two of them alone.

"JM, today I'm going to marry your Dad. Before I do, I want to make sure it's okay with you."

"It's okay with me. Do I get to call you Mother now?"

Tears filled her eyes as she said, "Is that what you want?"

"Yes, ma'am. I'll have the only mom that likes the same music as us kids."

Mandy laughed. "Is that right?"

"Yeah, all the other moms only like Elvis Presley, the Beatles and the Beach Boys."

Mandy was pleased to see how easily JM was adjusting to the situation. She handed him the gift and he quickly opened it. Excitement showed in his expression as he realized it was the latest video game. Grabbing it up, he said, "Can I go show Michael?"

"Sure, go ahead."

He turned at the door and said, "Thanks, Mom."

Mother had been hovering in the hallway listening to their conversation.

When JM came through the door she grabbed him up in her arms and said, "You're so sweet, I could eat you with a spoon."

"Ah, Mamaw. Let me go."

"Not until you give me some sugar."

"Michael says I'm too old to give you sugar."

"You tell Michael Wright that you are going to give me sugar until you're as old as your dad."

Squirming, he kissed her on the cheek and she let him go.

Watching them from the doorway, Mandy was overcome with emotion and said, "Now, Mother, look what you've done! Get in here and help me fix this makeup."

Reverend Harper began the ceremony with a brief history on how well he knew both individuals. He recounted how he had come out of retirement to join these two special people. He told the audience how he had done this for more than forty years and in his experience Jim and Mandy were meant for each other. He'd been talking for almost thirty minutes when an impatient Mandy said, "When do I get to say I do?"

Everyone laughed, including Reverend Harper. He said, "You get to talk right now." Five minutes later they were walking back down the aisle as husband and wife.

Mike yelled out at the top of his lungs from the back of the church, "Amen!"

After dinner, as the Wright family and the Barkleys watched the couple drive away for their honeymoon, Mike nuzzled Mother's neck and said, "Well, girl, looks like we finally got them married."

"Isn't that just like a man – the women do all the work and the men take the credit!"

Mike apologized quickly, realizing he'd stepped in it this time. "Mother, you know what I mean."

Still mad, she snapped, "Get in here and help me with all these dishes!"

Chapter 42

The Honeymoon

After three days, Mandy and Jim had explored every shop in Maggie Valley, North Carolina. It was a surprise to them that they were incapable of just relaxing. Each kept looking for something to do. Mandy found a brochure about the town of Helen, Georgia and showed it to Jim. "Have you ever been to Helen?"

"Is that the little German town northeast of Hiwassee?"

"According to this map, it's about 15 miles from there."

"I've heard of it, but never seen it. We should go there someday."

Excited, she said, "Let's go there today. I would love some German food. I haven't had any since my college days."

Surprised, Jim asked, "Have you been to Germany?"

Realizing that they had never discussed their travels, she said, "Many times. I went to Europe every summer while I was going to college. It was a special time for Dad and me. I'm sorry I didn't tell you about it before."

Smiling, he said, "You're one surprise after another. Next you'll tell me you've slept in the Grand Canyon."

She put her arms around his neck and gave him a peck on the cheek "More than once, my darling."

He turned and pulled her into his arms, laughing, and said, "I give up. Let's go to Helen."

It took them almost four hours on the winding mountain roads to reach their destination. It was as picturesque as the brochure had promised. Excited, Mandy said, "It's like someone dropped a little German village into the mountains of Georgia!"

After Jim parked the car they began to prowl the little shops. They stopped on the little bridge that crossed the small, mountain stream flowing through the middle of town. He said, "The brochure has pictures of people floating on inner tubes during the summer. I wonder if it has any trout. Maybe we can bring JM here next summer and give it a try."

Putting her arms around his waist, Mandy said, "What a wonderful idea. When we get home, have Shirley put it on your calendar so we can make it happen."

"Are you trying to tell me I'll forget?"

"Jim Coleman, don't go there."

Before he could reply, he noticed a sign on the restaurant across the street advertising the daily special of snow crab legs. "You know I haven't had crab legs since I was in San Francisco."

Mandy asked, "Have you ever had Chesapeake blue crab?"

"No, but they couldn't be better than snow crab legs."

"I guess that's something else we need to have Shirley put on your calendar. I can't be married to a man who doesn't know what real crab tastes like. Let's go look at the menu. Remember, we came for German food, not seafood."

"Can't we have both?"

"Of course. I hope all of our problems are as easily resolved."

He looked over the menu and said, "Well, I think I'm the hungriest. How about crab legs for lunch and German food for supper?"

"Well, okay, but only because we're standing in front of the place and I hate to see a man drool."

Later that evening when they had finished their German meal, Jim said, "You know, we may have to make this a quarterly tradition."

"What tradition?"

"A visit to Helen to have crabs and German food."

"Do you think they'll ever have a good restaurant in Blue Ridge?"

"No, their ambition now seems to be to become the fast food capital of the world. What's heartbreaking is that they are achieving their goal."

On their way home the next morning, Mandy started talking about the apartment. It was then that Jim realized she thought they'd be living there. He had just assumed they'd live with the Barkleys. He decided to attack the issue straight on by saying, "Actually, we've never talked about where we're going to live."

Smiling she said, "I wondered when you'd bring it up."

"You've been talking to Mother about this, haven't you?"

She laughed and said, "I cannot tell a lie. Yes, we discussed it."

"What did you two decide?"

"We decided it's up to you to solve the problem."

"I can see right now that you two are setting me up."

Chapter 43

Guidance

When Mandy and Jim stopped in front of the Barkley's house, JM was the first to see them. Jim had never seen him so excited. He almost jumped into his arms. Jim thought it was because he was so glad to see them, but the real reason came out quickly. "Daddy, I'm 11 now and Michael says I can join his Boy Scout troop. Can I? Can I, huh?"

Disappointed, Jim said, "We'll see."

The excitement drained from JM's face and body. It was like someone had stuck a hole in a basketball. It was still a basketball, but was now useless to play with. JM had heard 'We'll see' before and experience had taught him that it really meant no way! Mike heard Jim's answer and saw its effect on JM. After everyone had welcomed them home, Mike whispered to Jim, "Can I talk to you in private?"

Hearing the serious tone of Mike's voice, Jim said, "Sure, Mike, what's up?"

"Let's walk out to my new smokehouse."

"What's a smokehouse?"

"That's where people smoke meat to preserve it for winter, but I built it so I could have a place to store my garden tools."

"Why don't you call it a tool shed?"

Laughing, Mike said, "Smokehouse sounds more country, don't you think? But seriously, I heard what you said to the boy. Do you realize how hard it hit him?"

Confused, Jim said, "But I will see. Being a scout takes up a lot of time and I don't have it to give."

"You don't have it or it's just inconvenient for you?"

Mike's words hit Jim hard. Defensively, he said, "You know how busy I am."

Mike responded, "And whose fault is that?"

"I have to earn a living."

Mike placed his arm around Jim's shoulder and said, "Have you ever heard that it's the yeses that change our lives and not the no's?"

"I've never heard that before."

"It's true, trust me. But first let me tell you about how I learned that hard lesson as a father. When my Michael was about 13 he sold *Grits* and mowed lawns to earn a little money."

"What are grits?"

"*Grits* is a newspaper that comes out once a week that has all the top stories from the other major papers."

"That sounds like USA Today."

"Yeah, it's similar, but it only comes out once a week. I'm not sure, but I think Michael sold it for 25 cents. He kept ten cents and sent the rest back to the company. It was and is a wonderful business tool for young boys."

"Where's the hard lesson?"

"It's coming. At first he walked to sell the papers. One day a friend sold him a used bicycle for three dollars. It didn't have fenders or even a sprocket guard, but he was as proud of it as if it were brand new. Because he didn't tell me he was going to buy it, I lost my temper and made him return it and get his money back."

Wide-eyed, Jim asked, "Did he do it?"

"Yes, Michael always did what he was told."

"Why did you make him return it?"

Mike's eyes filled with tears. "You know, to this day I don't know why. But that was the wedge I drove between us. From that time on, he never shared his thoughts, goals or desires with me. He would tell his Mother when he did something he was proud of and then tell her when it was okay to tell me."

"Mike, I can't believe he'd do that to you. You're the most generous person I know."

"I'm afraid Michael felt I was a naysayer in his life. What hurts the most is that he was right. You know, I didn't even know he joined the Army until the morning he left. And I didn't know he was going to helicopter school until after he graduated."

"Why are you telling me this?"

"I want you to think about your own life. When did good things start happening to you? When you said yes or when you said no? If you'd said no to Peggy when she asked you to dance, where would you be now?"

Jim thought for a minute. "You're right, Mike. And I wouldn't even have JM. Looks like you're trying to tell me JM is going to be a scout."

Mike let out one of his big laughs. "Looks like you didn't fall off the turnip truck after all."

"I may be slow, but I do recognize good guidance when I get it." Jim hesitated for a moment and then continued, "Speaking of guidance, Mandy and I had a discussion on where we're going to live. Apparently, I was slow on the uptake. I think she and Mother had already had that discussion, but Mandy told me it was my problem to solve. You have any ideas?"

Laughing until he was almost crying, Mike said, "Do you want the long solution or the short solution?"

"What do you mean?"

"Well, I have a list of houses that would be just perfect for the three of you. The long solution is I have five you can look at. The short one is for you to look at number five first."

"Where's number five?"

"It's about 500 feet from where you're standing right now, on the corner. The Campbell's are moving to Alabama to be with their children. It's a 4 bedroom place on about 5 acres. It even has space for a small garden in the back. But what makes it so perfect is JM could still catch the bus here in front of our house and stay with us until you guys get home. Mother knows that the best place for him is to be with you and Mandy, but the thought of not seeing him every day would kill her."

"Do I pretend to look at the others first?"

"Hmm, you're learning quickly, my boy. Get in the car and we'll drive by the other places and later you can surprise them with your decision."

Chapter 44

Finding A Truck

It was the end of November already and Charlie still hadn't found a truck. Legs was nagging him to death. For some strange reason he didn't care. Looking for the right truck had become a passion for him. He couldn't wait for Friday evenings so he could continue his search. For more than a month he had only seen Legs late on Sunday nights. Her frustration just rolled off him like water off a duck's back. He was having fun and he didn't care how much she nagged him. Each weekend he pushed farther and farther into the mountains of Georgia. Many of the roads were still just dirt and every mile or so he had to forge a small stream. Finally, one day he followed one of the roads for over an hour and it emptied into a two-lane paved road. When he noticed a brand new street sign saying Boardtown Road, he was flooded with memories of spending weekends with his dad. It had always been such an adventure for him as a small boy to go on exciting road trips. He remembered once when his dad had taken him to see Old Chief Whitepath's cabin, and he suddenly felt an urge to see it again. He began to follow Boardtown Road until he saw something familiar. He turned off on a road he thought might lead him to the cabin, but was disappointed to come out on Highway 5 between Ellijay and Cherry Log. He pulled up behind a pickup when he saw two men cutting firewood.

Getting out of his car he walked over to the men and said, "Excuse me. I don't want to interrupt, but I need some directions."

The men stopped working and the older gentleman said, "No problem. Any excuse to rest is always welcome. What kind of directions do you need?"

"When I was a boy my father took me to Chief Whitepath's cabin. I just can't remember how we got there."

"Well, mister, you're nearly there, but you have a problem."

"What do you mean?"

The man pointed to an overgrown dirt road about a hundred yards away. "Down that road is where it was, but they moved it up to Blairsville."

"Blairsville? Are you serious?"

"Serious as a heart attack. They moved it lock, stock and barrel to some museum. If you want to see it again, you'll need to go there."

"I guess I'll do that some day. I was just thinking back to my childhood."

The younger cutter asked, "Who is this Chief Whitepath?"

His companion said, "Don't they teach you anything in school, boy? He was a famous Cherokee chief who went on the Trail of Tears."

"We read about that in school, but I didn't know it started here."

Charlie couldn't stay out of the conversation any longer. "My father told me that Chief Whitepath joined General Andrew Jackson in 1814 to fight the Creeks at the Battle of Horseshoe Bend in Alabama. Along with a small band of Cherokees, he stole the Creeks' canoes so they couldn't escape by water. The Chief thought he could go talk to his friend, President Jackson, and stop the removal of the Cherokees to Oklahoma. He was surprised when President Jackson turned out to be a fair-weather friend and sent them anyway. My father said the Chief died on the way to Oklahoma. He's buried where Ft. Campbell, Kentucky is now."

The younger man said, "You'd think Jackson would have taken care of him."

Charlie thought for a minute before commenting, "I asked my father why the president didn't help him. He said Jackson was a politician. They never do the right thing; they always do the easy thing."

The old cutter said, "I've never heard it put so plain. By God, that describes every politician I've ever known."

Charlie couldn't believe how much he was remembering about his father. His memories were wonderfully positive until his mother had died. After that, he could not remember having spent any time with him. All his father had done after her death was work morning and night until he died of a heart attack.

The bittersweet memories flooded his eyes with tears. Realizing where he was, he tried to regain his composure and turned to the wood cutters, "I thank you gentlemen, for your information. Good luck with your work."

"Don't need luck, just a strong back. Enjoyed talking with you. Come back and to see us, you hear?"

Charlie continued on his exploration of the back roads of North Georgia. Finally, late one Saturday he saw it. In front of an old farmhouse that had to have been built in the late 30s and had not received a fresh coat of paint since was a 1951 five-window, Chevrolet pickup with a 'For Sale' sign on it. The asking price simply stated, 'Make an Offer'. Charlie knew he had to have it. This special truck was what his father had always looked for but had never found. Upon closer inspection he could see why it had such a low price tag.

Over the years the owner had used it to haul fertilizer and salt for his farm. All the sheet metal, fenders, doors and truck bed were eaten away by rust. The farmer had welded strips of metal on the fenders to keep them attached. Looking under the truck, he saw the frame was rusty also. Some of it was eaten away where the bed joined the cab. He asked the owner if it ran. The owner turned on the ignition key, patted the accelerator two times and pushed the starter button. It came alive. He raced the engine and announced he had put in new points and plugs the previous summer.

Charlie asked, "What will you take for it?"

Seeing his big, fancy car, the farmer said, "I was offered $600 last week."

"Wow. That was a good price. Why didn't you take it?"

The farmer was prepared with a come back. "He didn't have but $200 cash and wanted to pay the rest on credit. It's all cash or no deal with me, mister."

"Well, I've got the cash, but I have a problem."

"What's that?" asked the farmer.

"I need to drive it to my shop in South Carolina and those tires won't make it."

"I can get you new tires for less than $100."

"If you can do that for me, I'll give you $800 cash."

With a satisfied grin the farmer said, "Mister, you've got a deal."

Pulling out eight $100 bills, Charlie asked, "When can I pick up my truck?"

"I'll give you the title today and you can pick it up next Saturday, if that's okay with you."

"That'll be fine."

He accepted the signed title and started home. He stopped at the first phone booth he saw and called Legs to tell her to meet him at his place because he had a big surprise for her.

Chapter 45

Picking Up The Truck

As the week went by, Charlie got more excited. It reminded him of the week before Christmas when his Mother was alive. It was almost 10:00 o'clock when Legs turned into his driveway. Before she could get out he opened the passenger side door of her car and said, "You're late, so you can drive."

"Well, hello to you, too. I guess I'm just chopped liver. No kiss, no I love you or I missed you?"

She could see how excited he was and was amused at this side of his personality. It was a pleasant change. She started the engine and asked, "Which way to this wonderful truck of yours?"

She drove, Charlie described to her how many weekends he and his father had spent looking for just this type of truck to restore.

For this first time she felt a little sorry for him and said, "I can't believe you and your dad weren't able to find one."

He sat for a moment and then said, "Oh, we found a couple, but at that time we couldn't afford them. Dad had just started his practice and it was all he could do to pay the rent and put food on the table." He turned towards her and said, "I didn't really understand until just a few days ago what it was like then. When I retraced the route Daddy and I took to Chief Whitepath's cabin I remembered him saying that one day he would have enough money for my mother to live in the style she deserved."

Legs didn't like the direction the conversation was taking. Finding this truck had put Charlie on a sentimental journey into his past that could derail all of her plans. "Charlie, are you saying you don't want to be a Senator anymore?"

Surprised he said, "I want it even more now. I also remember that it was Daddy that was going to be the Senator. It was because of his weak heart that my uncle took the seat Daddy earned. My daddy died the day they swore my uncle in. I'm glad he's finally in the graveyard. When they make me a Senator I will dedicate it to my father."

Relieved that Charlie was more determined than ever, she asked, "How much farther on this old dirt road?"

"We're nearly there. When you cross the next stream it will be the first house on the left."

When she pulled up next to the old truck, Charlie said, "He did it. See the new tires?"

She stared in disbelief at the condition of the old truck. "Are you sure it won't fall apart before we get home?"

"No, it might look rough, but it's okay. Farmers actually use their trucks. They don't care what they look like as long as they get the job done."

"Trust me, this farmer really didn't care how it looked. Just get the key and let's get out of here."

"You turn around and I'll go tell him we're in a big hurry, or he'll want us to come in and have coffee. See that cup in his hand? I'll bet he wants to brag about how hard he had to work to get those new tires in order to live up to his end of the deal."

Shaking her head, she thought, *Men are all alike. They want praise for every little thing they do.* She said, "Tell him I've got a sick mother at home and that we have to go."

"I'll be back as soon as I can. Give me a minute."

In just a few minutes Charlie returned and placed his hand on the top of the car. "He said he hopes your mom gets better soon. Follow me; I think I know a quicker way home."

"Okay, but hurry up. Let's go."

Talking Rock

Charlie slid in the front seat of the truck. He couldn't believe how big the steering wheel was. It seemed twice as large as the one on his Mercedes. He turned the key and the engine jumped to life. It sounded good and he could feel the power under his foot. It had been a long time since he had driven a stick shift, but he quickly remembered the truck's gears. He was surprised at hard how it was to steer and could now see why the wheel was so large. Without power steering, you needed all of the mechanical advantage you could get. He could see Legs following him about a hundred feet back. She was trying to stay out of the dust cloud he was making with the truck. Just ahead he saw the dirt road leading to Boardtown Road; he turned right onto the paved road and shifted into high gear. As he traveled he noticed a roaring noise coming from the left front tire. He speeded up and the noise got louder. By the time he got up to 35 mph the entire front end of the truck began to shimmy. At 45 mph it was all he could do to keep it on the road. He decided he'd better pull over and stop. Legs pulled up behind him and yelled, "What's wrong? Are you out of gas?"

"I've got gas, but when I get up to 45 mph the front end shimmies so bad I can't hold it in the road."

"What are we going to do?"

"We need to get the front end aligned."

"Why? We're going to wreck it anyway."

"I can only get up to 35 or 45 mph. That's not enough speed to force anybody off the road, much less get them killed."

She looked around and asked, "Where?"

"The closest town is Ellijay. We need to find a tire shop. They usually do alignments."

"Can you make it that far?"

"If I drive about 30 mph, I think it'll be okay."

She followed the slow truck to Ellijay. She had never been so glad to see any town in her life. Charlie pulled into the first business he saw. It was a feed and seed store. He ran inside and when he came out he said, "The guy said there's a shop on Main Street just as you leave town on the south side. He said if we see the river on the left, we've gone too far."

As they crept through town he saw the tire shop the guy had described. He pulled the truck up to an open bay and went inside. He described the symptoms to the manager. "The roaring noise sounds like a wheel bearing. I'll need to pull that wheel to see. Can't do it today though. See those cars out there? They're all ahead of you."

"If I leave it with you, can you fix it next week?"

"Sure, but do you want to waste good money on it? It looks like it's on its last legs."

"I know, but me and my boy are going to fix it up."

The manager laughed. "Hope he's a young boy, cause it's going to take you a long time."

Charlie thought, *How nice it would have been to share this with Daddy.* Smiling, he said, "We're not in any rush, so fix it right when you do it."

"I can't get to it until Tuesday. If you give me your number I'll call you when I find out what it needs."

Charlie lied and said, "I'm going on a business trip to Orlando next week. Can I just call you on Wednesday morning?"

He handed Charlie his card and said, "That'll be fine. I'll be here all day except at lunch."

Charlie walked out to where Legs was waiting in the car. "They can't get to it until next week. Do you like barbecue?"

"I love it, why?"

"I thought since we were so close we could drive up to Cherry Log and eat at the Pink Pig."

She smiled, "If it's good enough for Jimmy Carter, I think it's good enough for a victory celebration."

"What victory celebration?"

"You got the truck, didn't you? That's a major step in our plan to make you a Senator." She could see the change in his demeanor and thought, *Charlie's easier to read than a comic book.*

Talking Rock

The following Wednesday Charlie forced himself to wait until 10:00 o'clock before he made the call. A young boy answered, "Tire shop."

Charlie asked, "May I speak with the manager?"

"Sure thing. He's under a car, so give me a minute."

Charlie could hear the manager's footsteps over the phone. He said, "How can I hep ya?"

"I'm the owner of the 51 Chevy truck."

"Oh, yeah. I was right about your wheel bearings. They're shot. Did you know the rim on the left tire is bent?"

"No, I didn't."

"Do you have a spare? We couldn't find one on the truck."

Embarrassed, Charlie said, "I'm not sure. When I bought it, I didn't check."

"I can get a used one at the junk yard down the street. Shouldn't cost more than ten bucks."

"That'll be fine. What will all of it cost me?"

"Well, I recommend we put bearings on the other side, too. One of your wheel cylinders is also leaking. You need a brake job before you take her back on the road."

"I agree. Can you do all that before Saturday?"

"Sure can. I think I can get it all done for about $300-$350."

Charlie was pleased to hear they could get it in running order so quickly. "That sounds good. Do what's needed and don't let the cost stop you from working. I have a budget of about $500."

"It won't take that much. I was just afraid you'd change your mind about putting that much money in that old truck."

Charlie understood what the manager was saying. He was probably used to customers telling him they could get it done cheaper somewhere else. So many people seemed to have the mindset *Don't do it right, just do it cheap.*

Chapter 46

The Fbi

Mark was sitting at the temporary desk assigned to him while he was attached to GBI when Walter brought in an obvious-- based on the way he was dressed-- FBI agent.

"Mark, this is Agent Tom Jones, from the FBI."

He was a big man with a big smile. "Mark, don't stand up. I'm going to be in the area all day. Before you ask, I'm not the singer."

Mark liked him from the start. He was the first FBI agent he had ever met that actually seemed human.

"I was sent over here to help you boys and claim all the credit for solving this case for the Bureau." Then he laughed again.

Mark's facial expression showed signs of worry.

Agent Jones turned to Walter and said, "Walt? I can call you Walt, can't I?"

Caught off guard, Walter realized no one had ever called him that. Even in school he was always called Walter. He liked the sound of Walt and he liked this agent. "Sure, if I can call you Tom."

"That's a deal. Do we call Word, Kind? No, Nasty is more appropriate for him."

They laughed, although Mark didn't see the humor.

"Seriously, guys. I'm here to help. I reviewed all your reports last week and it looks like you have done a top-notch investigation. I took the liberty of doing a computer search for crimes involving a father and son with the weapon being a Springfield 03. I began the search in 1970, which is as far back as our data goes. I found 7 cases; 5 in Georgia and 2 in Alabama. All but one was listed as a murder/suicide. The one exception was a case where a woman killed her father and brother. She was executed five years ago. The Gibson case makes number 8. It looks like we might really have a serial killer. That's why I'm here; not because a State Senator was killed. That information is just for you guys. I hate politicians and I didn't want you to think I was here because the Governor had called. Let's not tell the Governor, though, okay?" Then he laughed.

His candor relaxed Walter and Mark. It made him welcome to their team. He'd shared information he didn't need to with them. This guy was good. In less than an hour he had become a trusted member.

Walter asked, "Tom, we've about run out of leads. Do you have any ideas?"

"Not really. I have a couple questions. Let's review the evidence and maybe we'll come up with something. You have an informant that predicted the murders. You have her fingerprints. Her prints were also found at another crime scene. The rifle that killed the son at the first crime scene was the same rifle that killed the Judge and the Senator. They were both killed with the same bullet. It appears we really did have a serial killer in the 70's. He stopped killing for ten years and began again last year. There has to be a reason. My first question is: Why do you think the Senator was the primary target?"

Walter answered, "Because of the fact that he was killed at his home."

"I agree. That's a good premise. We have a lot of indicators that our killer is back. Is there anything that says it might not be him?"

Walter answered, "Well, in the Gibson case they were both killed with Springfield 03's, but it was two different rifles. Also, the killing of the Senator was the first time the killer used the same rifle in two separate murders."

"Great observation, Walt. You're good."

"Thanks."

"What concerns me is that the Senator's death doesn't fit the profile of a father and son. Could the killer have thought Judge Foster was the son?"

"Could be. He was 150 yards away."

Tom corrected him. "142 yards, by my notes."

Walter was impressed. Tom acted carefree; however, he was very precise in his investigation. Thinking out loud he said, "We figured Cagle was in the wrong place at the wrong time, but we hadn't thought that maybe the Judge was in the wrong place also. If that's true, do you think his son is still a target?"

"Could be, but I doubt it. The killer has had more than four months to correct his mistake and he hasn't. Also according to your informant the killer is now out of the state."

"Do you think he is?" asked Tom.

"No, I don't. She tried too hard to convince that reporter he was gone. What I do feel is that he's gone underground for a while until we stop the investigation."

Walter banged his hand on the desk in frustration and continued, "We can't let him get away."

"Walt, with Nasty's help we should solve this case in five notes. Oops, wrong game. What do you think, Nasty?"

Word reluctantly answered, "I hope so."

Tom turned his back to Word and said, "Walt, can you take me out to the ambush site? I need to walk the ground."

Walter stood up and grabbed his coat. "Sure, we can leave right now."

Chapter 47

Recon The Route

Legs laughed at how Charlie reacted to driving the old, beat-up truck. You would have thought he was driving a Rolls Royce. He quickly moved into the character of a farmer, throwing up his hand as he passed people on the road. What surprised her most was that everyone always waved back. *I never have understood why these country people wave like they know you*, she thought.

When they got the truck back to Charlie's house she had him put it in the garage and close the door. After that was taken care of, she decided they should make a recon of the route from Cartersville to Talking Rock. She began to get a little frustrated after a few miles as the road was narrow with a lot of sharp curves, but they couldn't seem to find a place that would cause major damage to an automobile forced off the road.

For the first time Charlie seemed to take control. "Relax, I know just the place. It's just around the curve."

As they rounded the curve she saw an old metal bridge across the river. There were steep drop offs at both ends of the bridge. Charlie suggested, "I was thinking just as she gets to the bridge. What do you think?"

Legs was speechless. She couldn't believe he had such a perfect plan. "Oh, Charlie. It's wonderful. I can't believe it. It's so perfect."

Charlie had a smile from ear to ear. Building on his success, he drove across the bridge for about 500 feet and then turned down a dirt path. This was the route the locals used to get to the river. He stopped on the bank of the river and pointed to where the water had washed out part of the bank. "That hole is about 15 feet deep. We can drive the truck in there and no one will ever find it."

I've created a monster, she thought. Returning his smile, she said, "Charlie, you're going to make a wonderful Senator."

"I know. Let's go to the Red Lobster on Peach Street and celebrate."

"Why not, Senator Webb."

Chapter 48

Trial Run

Legs was watching television with such interest that Charlie couldn't get her attention. He called out in a loud voice, "What are you watching?"

"Shhh. The weather."

After sitting quietly for another couple of minutes, she finally spoke.

"It looks like this is the week. Rain with possible chances of snow all next week. Clearing on Friday. If it snows, will your aunt still go to Talking Rock?"

"I think so. I heard her tell Lisa she hadn't missed a planned trip in two years."

"Is Wednesday her planned trip?"

"Yes. I made a copy of her calendar while she was out of the office. Wednesday is her second visit this month."

"Good. I'll take Wednesday off and go with you. This will be our first trial run."

"What do you mean by trial run?"

"Just that. We can't afford to have witnesses. If there are any other cars nearby when we get to the bridge we'll have to wait."

"I never thought of that. I've traveled that road many times, but have only seen a few cars."

"We can't afford to have even one car there when it happens. What time does she make the trip?"

"Usually between 9 and 9:30 a.m."

"Good. We'll have time to drop off your car first."

Puzzled, he asked, "My car?"

"How do you expect us to get back after we drive the truck into the river?"

Charlie didn't say a word. He hadn't thought of that and right now he wished he hadn't asked. Trying to sound smart, he suggested, "We need to find a place on the highway. With the rain and snow we could get stuck on that dirt path." He could tell Legs hadn't thought of that and he felt redeemed.

She asked, "Do you have a place in mind?"

"Yes, there's a picnic area off the side of the road about a half mile from the bridge. The roads are all graveled so we don't have to worry about getting stuck."

"Good, that's where we'll put the car in the morning."

At 7 a.m. Wednesday morning Legs knocked on Charlie's door. Her arms were filled with two large bags.

Charlie opened the door and asked, "What do you have there?"

"I thought we'd probably be sitting in that old, cold truck for a while, so I brought some snacks and a couple of Thermos bottles full of hot coffee."

The trip back to the site seemed shorter to Legs. About a mile from the bridge, Charlie pulled off the road into a driveway.

Legs asked, "Is this safe?"

"Oh yeah. This house has been abandoned for years."

Again she was impressed with Charlie's planning. "Here, have a cup of coffee, my future Senator."

Charlie's chest expanded with pride. At nine a.m. he started the truck. Surprised by the action she asked, "Do you see her?"

"Not yet, but I think we'd better keep this old truck ready to go."

"Me, too. Besides, I'm getting cold."

Twenty minutes later he saw his aunt driving towards them. As soon as she passed the driveway he pulled out onto the highway. Not being used to a stick shift, he missed the correct gear and the truck stalled.

Legs lost it. "Hurry! You're going to lose her."

Charlie started the truck and raced the engine. In an effort to catch his aunt he tried to get the maximum speed out of each gear. When he hit third gear he was only two hundred yards from her car and about a half mile from the bridge.

Legs began to direct him, "That's good, Charlie. Hold your speed and you should catch her right at the bridge."

Then without warning a teenager in a jacked-up truck with a roll bar full of lights came up behind them. Seeing how old Charlie's truck was, the teenager's pride wouldn't let him follow it. He downshifted and accelerated, quickly passing Charlie.

Legs continued with her non-stop coaching. "Don't worry about him. He'll pass her and be gone before we get there."

The teenager had the same idea until he got close enough to pass the Senator's car. Just as he began to pull around her he saw the special state license plates. He realized this was an important person and quickly pulled in behind her and followed at a legal distance.

Seeing this, Charlie said, "He didn't pass and I don't think he's going to."

"I know. I can see that," answered Legs. "Let's go back to your car. I need to get warm."

When they got back to the car Legs' teeth were chattering, caused primarily by the cold but assisted by the close encounter with the Senator. She suggested they drive over to the truck stop on I-75 near Cartersville to get something to eat and to get warm. In agreement, they decided they could return later to get the truck.

Chapter 49

Second Attempt

After being in the truck stop for an hour, both had finally warmed up. While there it began to rain. One of the customers came in shaking the rain from his hat and said, "It's sleeting out there. If this keeps up there'll be a lot of wrecks."

The waitress answered, "Can't wait to use that new wrecker, can you, Luther?"

"A fellow's gotta make a living."

Legs whispered, "Did you hear that? How long does your aunt stay with her sister?"

"I think about three to four hours. Why?"

"Then we still have time to get back to the truck. We could take her out on the way back. This is a perfect day. We have everything ready. Let's just do it."

They quickly paid the bill and drove back to the truck. They decided to use the picnic area to wait. Legs asked, "How much gas do you have?"

"We've got a full tank, why?"

"Good. Then keep the truck running and the heater on. I don't want to get cold again."

They sat for more than an hour watching the rain slowly turn from sleet to snow. Legs announced impatiently, "The weather is perfect. I wish she'd come by here soon."

Just when they both began to think they couldn't wait another minute, the Senator's car appeared in front of them. She was driving very slowly towards the bridge. Charlie pulled out onto the highway and began to follow her. He began to worry about her speed. "At the rate she's going I don't think forcing her off the road will get the job done. What can we do?"

Legs agreed and thought out loud, "If you speed up and hit her do you think it'll work?"

"It might, but I'd have to be doing more than sixty mph."

"Will this old truck go that fast?"

"Oh yeah. I'm just not sure whether I can keep her on the road in all this snow."

"Her? Next you'll tell me this truck has a name."

"Betsy."

"You do know we're putting Betsy in the river."

"I know. It's just I always wanted a truck I could call Betsy."

"Get over it. Slow down and give her a head start."

Charlie slowed down to about 20 mph. After about five minutes he began to speed up. When he reached 50 mph, he held it.

Legs asked, "Is this fast enough?"

"No, but if I go any faster I'll catch her before she gets to the bridge."

He smiled. Legs saw something strange in his face. It looked like pure satisfaction. Then without warning he pushed the accelerator to the floor and the old truck gained speed. Charlie was gripping the steering wheel with an evil grin on his face. Legs had never seen this side of him. He scared her. She could see the timing was going to be perfect. They would both arrive on the bridge at the same time.

Thinking out loud, Charlie said "I'll pass her at the last minute, and then make a sharp right turn into her left front tire. The impact should drive her over the bridge and into the river."

Excited, Legs yelled, "**Do it. Do it!** "

The Senator was already nervous from driving in the falling snow. She was constantly checking her mirrors. Seeing the old pickup coming, she began to worry about the bridge. It seemed to be coming on fast and she just hoped it would pass her before she drove onto the bridge. It was narrow and she didn't like having to pass a car on it. She made a promise to herself. If she made it across the bridge safely, she would find another route to her sister's house.

Just as Charlie had planned, they both hit the edge of the bridge together. He began to pass her car. Quickly his front bumper was in line with the front door of her car. Another two feet and he would turn into her. Unconsciously, he was gradually getting closer to her car. That scared his aunt and she stepped on the brakes in the instant before Charlie turned into her car. The truck turned quickly to the right; however, there was no front tire to hit. The Senator could see she was going to hit the right side of the bridge and instinctively she turned the wheel to the left. Her actions caused her car's front bumper to hit just short of the right rear fender of the truck. With this bump the truck slid in the direction of the major steel beam of the bridge. Seeing that her action had caused her to hit the truck, she overcorrected to the right. The force of her car hitting the bridge brought it to a sudden stop. She was slammed against the driver's door and window with the impact. The glass exploded, cutting both her left shoulder and head. Her face was quickly covered in blood. As the blood dripped into her eyes she went into shock. She kept repeating, "He tried to run me off the bridge."

Because Charlie had continued to maintain his speed, the truck hit the steel beam of the bridge dead center. The impact pushed the engine and transmission back into the cab with Legs and Charlie. As the engine slid to the rear it pushed the steering column into Charlie's chest. The force knocked him unconscious. For what seemed an eternity, Legs kept hearing tires squealing, glass breaking and metal twisting. Then it was over. She was wedged into her corner of the cab. She felt something warm on her face. She thought it must be Charlie's blood because she didn't hurt anywhere. She asked, "Charlie, are you alright?"

Regaining consciousness, Charlie could smell a familiar smell he remembered from his childhood. It was engine oil burning on a hot engine block. He thought, *The valves cover gasket must be leaking. I need to fix that.*

Looking at Legs, he said, "You look horrible. Why are you so pale? Don't worry; it's over now. When do you think they'll make me a Senator?"

Before she could answer he began to cough up blood.

"Legs, I think I'm hurt." Those were his last words.

She saw him slump over. "Charlie, wake up. We've got to drive the truck into the river." Just before she lost consciousness, she realized she had no feeling from her chest down.

Chapter 50

The Police Report

Walter walked into Mark's office. "Get your coat, we've got to go."

"What's up?" he asked.

"Someone tried to kill Senator Webb."

"Where? When?"

"About an hour ago on a bridge near Talking Rock."

Putting on his coat, Mark asked, "Which bridge?"

"That old metal bridge between Cartersville and Talking Rock."

"I know that bridge. The best route will be up I-75. What about Tom?"

"He said he'd meet us there."

When they arrived, it looked like a police parking lot. Walter asked the first officer he came upon, "Who's in charge?"

Pointing, he said, "That man over there chewing gum."

Chewing gum was an understatement. He was chewing it as if it were his last meal. Walter asked, "Are you in charge?"

"Hmmm. I guess I am. I'm Sheriff Don Queen. How can I help you boys?"

"I'm Agent Walter Rogers." He showed him his badge. "This is Tom Jones and Mark Word."

Shaking their hands, the sheriff said, "GBI, huh? What's your interest?"

Putting his badge away, Walter said, "I'm the leader of a task force that's investigating the previous Senator Webb's murder. We heard someone forced his wife off the road."

"That's what she keeps repeating, but it looks to me like the accident was just caused by inclement weather. Look for yourself. I think this old farmer boy tried to pass her on the bridge and lost control. He hit that center beam. The steering wheel really messed him up."

Walter, seeing the driver's side of the truck was cut away and the seat was empty, asked, "Where is he now?"

"That's him over there in the body bag. His missus is still trapped in the truck."

"Why didn't they take him with the Senator?"

"Would you believe they can't haul a dead body and an injured person in the same ambulance? That's their rule. Rules are going to be the death of this nation. You know, I'll bet one day they'll have a rule where you can't smoke in the courthouse."

"Sheriff, how many accidents has the weather caused?"

"This is only the second one for us today."

"How can you account for that? We must have seen five or six on our way here from Atlanta."

"These country folks just stay home when there's bad weather. Only fools try to go out in this." He started chewing his gum again.

Smiling, Walter said, "I guess that includes us."

Moving his gum to the side of his mouth, he answered, "We're a little different. It's our job, but I have to admit I do feel foolish every time I hit a patch of ice."

He began to chew again and pulled a pack of gum from his pocket. "Would you boys like some gum? My wife is making me give up smoking. My new year's resolution to quit has been the same every year we've been married; however, this year my sweetie put her foot down. She's only five foot tall but she sure has a big foot." He laughed. "She said if I kept smoking, I'd die and leave her, so she decided if I didn't stop she'd just leave me first."

Smiling, Walter said, "Sounds like she's serious."

"Oh my God, yes. She even makes spot checks all times of the day and night. God, I love that woman. Here take a piece."

Accepting a piece, Walter asked, "When do you think they'll get the wife out?"

"I'm not sure. The farmer was dead when we arrived, so they just used a cutting torch to cut him out. They can't do that with her. I heard the fire chief tell someone to go to Fulton County to get their jaws of life. That's an expensive piece of equipment our county can't afford."

While Walter and the Sheriff were talking, Tom and Mark moved closer to the truck to survey the damage. They were looking through where the driver's door had been when Legs opened her eyes. Not seeing Charlie, she asked, "Where's Charlie? Did he go and get the car?"

Tom asked, "Where's the car?"

"Why, it's parked in the picnic area, of course."

Looking at Tom for a minute, she asked, "Who are you?"

"Tom Jones, at your service."

"Tom Jones? This is wonderful. Can I have your autograph?"

"Sure, what's your name?"

"Sue, but you can call me Legs. My friends..." Her eyes closed as she lost consciousness.

Tom went to the Sheriff. "The lady in the truck said they have a car parked in the picnic area. Is there one nearby, or is she just delirious?"

The Sheriff answered, "No, there's one about a half mile down the road. I'll send one of the deputies to check."

Walter asked, "Do you know who the farmer was?"

"I've got his belongings in the car. Let me get them."

Returning, he pulled out the driver's license. "His name is Charles D. Webb. He lives here in Cartersville."

Walter couldn't believe his ears. "Did you say Charles Webb?"

Handing the driver's license to Walter, the sheriff said, "Yeah. You know him?"

Looking at the picture on the license, Walter said, "He's the Senator's nephew."

The sheriff said, "He sure looked like just another farm boy to me."

Seeing the humor in the sheriff's words, Walter laughed and said, "No, in fact he was a lawyer in Cartersville and the Senator's assistant."

A deputy ran up to the Sheriff saying, "Bobby said there's a car in the parking lot registered to a Charles Webb."

The sheriff thanked the deputy then turned to Walter and Mark. "Boys, I think we need to go check this out."

Tom stepped up. "Sheriff, I'm with the FBI." He showed him his badge. "I'll take over now."

The Sheriff's mouth dropped open and the gum he was chewing fell to the ground. "FBI? What the hell?"

Giving the sheriff a short answer, Tom said, "We think this guy is a serial killer. Do you have his car keys in that bag?"

With his mouth still wide open the sheriff handed the bag to Tom and said, "Here's everything on the body. I'm not sure about keys."

"Thanks, Sheriff. Can you have your deputy secure the area? I can have a team there in a couple of hours."

"Sure can. You know, I've never worked with the FBI before. Do you mind if I tag along? If it gets around I worked with the FBI, it could help me come election time."

Smiling, Tom said, "Always willing to help a fellow cop."

Once again Tom had charmed someone into being a supportive member of the team.

Chapter 51

Finding The Killer

Tom went into Walter's office to give him an update. "Walt, it looks like we found our killer. The team found a lot of incriminating evidence.

Walter was excited. "Good, solid evidence?"

"I would think so. They found two Springfield rifles. One was the rifle that killed Cagle, Judge Foster and the Senator. They also found $250,000 in a wall safe in his office. Ben Gibson's prints were all over the bag and the money."

Standing and placing his hands in the middle of his desk, Walter asked, "What about the woman?"

Reading from a file, Tom said, "Her prints prove she was the tall, blond you've been looking for."

Reaching for the file, Walter asked, "What does she say about all this?"

Tom said, "She hasn't regained consciousness yet. Last I heard, she was on the operating table. The gearshift went through her stomach and abdomen. The fireman just cut it off at the base and the doctors are trying to remove it now. I thought we could go over later when she's awake and ask her some questions."

Almost eight hours later, Legs regained consciousness.

The doctor said to Tom, "You can talk to her now, but I don't think she'll make any sense. I'd recommend you wait until tomorrow."

Walter looked at Tom and asked, "What do you think?"

"I guess we can wait one more day. Who is she anyway?" asked Tom.

Reading from his notebook Walter said. "Her name is Sue McGill. She's a teacher in Blue Ridge and a single parent with two boys."

Shaking his head, Tom said, "Makes you wonder how she ever got mixed up with a killer."

Walking away, Walter said, "Maybe she'll clear that up for us tomorrow."

Chapter 52

I Want A Lawyer

Thursday morning Legs woke with a horrible headache. She didn't know where she was.

The nurse sitting by her bed noticed her open her eyes. "Good morning, sleepyhead," she said. "We didn't think you'd ever wake up."

Legs mumbled, "Where am I? What happened?"

Checking her pulse, the nurse said, "You're in Grady Memorial Hospital. You were in a car accident."

Seeing it was light outside, Legs asked, "What time is it?"

The nurse looked at her watch and said, "It's about 9:30 a.m."

"I'm late for work. I have to get out of here." She was suddenly scared as she tried to move. She realized she could only lift her head. The rest of her body refused to work.

Pushing her head gently back against the pillows, the nurse said, "Just relax. They know you'll be here a while. Lay back and rest." She pushed the call button and when another nurse appeared, she asked, "Would you please tell Dr. George she's awake?"

Shortly thereafter, the doctor came into the room. "How are you feeling this morning?"

"I have a horrible headache and I feel numb all over."

Looking at her chart, the doctor said, "That's the medication. You gave us a real scare last night. Try to get a little more rest and I'll be back in a few hours."

When the doctor left the room, Legs asked, "How long have I been here? Where are my boys?"

Trying to calm her down, the nurse said, "The ambulance brought you in last night. I think your boys are in the waiting room."

Excited, she asked, "Can I see them?"

"For a couple of minutes, but only if you promise to stay very still. I don't want you to pull out your stitches."

While the boys were visiting with their mom, the doctor notified Walter she was awake. Within the hour, Tom, Walter and Mark were in the waiting room. The doctor warned he didn't think she would remember anything about the accident.

Walter asked, "How is she?"

Talking in a very low voice, the doctor said, "She's really in bad shape. We had to amputate her left leg below the knee, but that's not what concerns me. We had to remove a steel rod from her abdomen that nicked her backbone. Right now she's paralyzed. Both small and large intestines were punctured. I think we found all the damage, but we'll know for sure by tomorrow."

"If you didn't, what then?" Walter asked.

"Infection will set in. The worst part will be if there are any leaks. If there are, the poison will spread throughout her system."

"That sounds serious," said Walter. "What happens then?"

"If they're not found and fixed it will eventually kill her."

Realizing that she might die, Walter asked, "What are her chances?"

The doctor was slow to answer. "Less than fifty-fifty, but if we can get her through the weekend, she should be okay."

Moving in front of the doctor, Tom asked, "Can we talk to her now?"

"Yes, but try not to upset her if you can."

Tom walked into the room and showed her his badge. "I'm Agent Jones and would like to ask you a few questions if I could."

The first thing that came to Legs' mind was that they had traced her call. Meekly she answered, "I'm not saying anything until my lawyer is here."

Walter quickly said, "We're not charging you with anything. We just need some information about your friend, Charles Webb."

Legs face flushed. "Go ask Charlie. Leave me alone. I'm not saying anything without my lawyer."

Tom kept his voice calm. "Do you remember anything about the accident?"

Getting upset she said, "I told you, get my lawyer first."

Fighting frustration and trying hard to please her, Tom asked, "Who is your lawyer?"

"Jim Coleman in Blue Ridge. He'll answer your questions."

Walter couldn't believe what he was hearing. Again he wondered if Jim was involved. Tom excused himself, thanked her for her patience and told her they wouldn't come back until her lawyer was present. Back in the waiting room, Tom asked, "Walt, wasn't Coleman your number one suspect?"

"Yes, he was."

Shaking his head, Tom said, "Just when I thought everything was going to be so clean, shit hits the fan."

Opening his notebook, Walter said, "I have his phone number. I'll get him down here today."

"Good, I think we better act quickly. From what that doctor said, I don't think she's going to make it."

Chapter 53

The Story

The first person Jim and Sam saw when they entered the waiting room was Walter who immediately told them about the accident and the discovery of the weapons that killed the Senator. Walter stated that the FBI had enough evidence to prove Charlie had killed all three men. They also knew that Sue was involved but were not sure to what extent. Walter wanted to know how Jim knew Sue.

Jim explained the connection. "Sue was a close friend of my first wife, Peggy and I also represented her son, Johnny, last year. What can I do?"

Tom, who was listening, answered for Walter. "We don't think she carried out any of the killings; therefore, if she will provide us with information we won't charge her."

Jim requested that promise in writing. Tom complied. When they entered Sue's room, Jim was shocked to see the ghostly woman lying in the bed. "Sue, what did you do to yourself?"

Barely audible, she labored out, "Oh, Jim. I really screwed up this time."

Barely able to hear her, Jim leaned closer as she continued, "My boyfriend, Charlie, has got us in bad trouble. I was wondering if you could represent us."

Looking at Walter, Jim said, "She doesn't know yet?"

Walter whispered, "No."

"Know what?" whispered Sue.

Jim said, "Charlie was killed in the accident."

Straining, she answered, "That little bastard! All that work and he dies on me." Gasping for air she asked, "What am I going to do?"

"Sue, this FBI agent has proven that Charlie was responsible for Senator Webb's death. He has given me a written statement that if you will cooperate they won't charge you with anything."

Weakly she asked, "Jim, what do you think?"

"I recommend you tell them everything. Charlie's dead and he can't hurt you anymore."

Breathing deeply, she saw her way out of the mess she was in, and began to slowly tell her story, implying that everything had been Charlie's idea.

When questioned about the serial killer she explained how on one of her visits to the jail Peggy told her Jim was trying to get her out of jail by blaming the Fosters' death on a serial killer. When she had repeated the story to Charlie, he decided he would copy cat the serial killer. They asked and she verified that's why he had killed Ben Gibson and his son first. She was shocked when Walter asked why they used two rifles for the Gibson killing. She responded by saying she wasn't sure, but she knew he had killed the son in the morning and the father late that afternoon. When asked if she was there she said it was during the week and she was probably teaching. They decided not to pursue it. She went on to say that Charlie wanted to kill his uncle so he could become his replacement in the Senate. In response to their questions about why he would have killed the Judge and the deputy, she said it was to prevent Judge Foster from being recommended as the Senator's successor. Judge Foster had become a very important person to his aunt because he had helped get her son out of a mess.

Then they asked her about the accident. She explained that Charlie was upset that his aunt had replaced her husband instead of letting him fill the seat. He methodically planned her death. To ensure that he would be the obvious choice to replace her, he became her personal assistant. He knew an accident was the only way to get her out of the way without becoming a suspect himself. She tried to deflect any suspicions they might have about her part of the plan by telling the agents that she had tried to call Bill Dean and warn them. She told them he wouldn't listen to her and concluded her story with, "That's all I know. When can I get out of here?"

Tom tactfully said, "That'll be up to your doctor. We have everything we need. Thank you so much. You get well now."

Chapter 54

Hospital Room

That afternoon the doctor asked Jim to join him when he explained to Sue just how sick she really was. When he had finished, Sue just stared at him. The doctor told her he needed someone to sign paperwork giving them permission to operate again. He went on to explain her declining condition was evidence that they had not repaired all the damage. Then he asked her who could give permission for further medical treatment if she became incapacitated. Listening and seeing the impact this news was having on Sue, Jim felt helpless.

Tears filled her eyes as she said, "I have no one."

The doctor asked if there was someone she could appoint as her power of attorney.

She looked at Jim and said, "Would you do that for me?"

"Sue, you were there for Peggy. Yes, of course I will. Just tell me exactly what you want done."

That night he called Mandy and explained what was going on and asked if she could come down Saturday and stay until Sunday. He explained that Sue was critical and he couldn't leave until the crisis was over. Mandy was sorry about the circumstances, but she was happy Jim wanted her there.

Shortly after she reached the hospital, Mandy met with Sue's doctor. As a professional courtesy they explained they had done all they could and that she would probably expire within hours. Mandy went to the waiting room. She pulled Jim aside and broke the awful news. They returned to comfort the boys.

Just as they sat down, Senator Webb walked into the hospital waiting room. Seeing a group of people together, she asked, "Are you Mrs. McGill's family?"

Mandy walked up and said, "I'm Dr. Hicks. The two boys are her sons. Can I help you?"

"I just wanted to talk with Mrs. McGill. I was hoping she could explain why Charlie would want me dead."

Mandy answered, "She's unconscious and the doctors here tell me that they don't expect her to live until morning."

Overhearing their conversation, Jim moved Mandy and the Senator into the hallway. Addressing her he said, "I think he wanted to take your place as Senator."

"That's what it's all about? Charlie wanted to be Senator? I hate the job. If he had asked he could have had it. Excuse me, but who are you?"

"Sorry, ma'am, I'm Jim Coleman, a friend of Sue's family."

Recognizing the name, she asked, "Are you the Jim Coleman that refused to take my son's case?"

His face flushed a bright red as he said, "I'm afraid so, ma'am."

With a slight smile she said, "At first I was upset with you, but now I realize it took guts to refuse my husband. I respect that."

Pleased with her answer, Jim said, "Thank you, ma'am."

"After his mother died everyone spoiled and pampered Charlie. He was never required to work or earn anything. He died trying to get something that would easily have been his if he had only tried to earn it. I've learned an important lesson today. I've been on the fence about sending Brent to Fork Union Military School in Virginia. His life of easy living is over. It's going to be military school in winter and work as a bag boy at my sister's grocery store during the summer. Mr. Coleman, do you have children?"

"Yes, ma'am, one boy."

"Learn from this tragedy and practice tough love."

Talking Rock

"Yes, ma'am. I think I understand what you're saying."

Mandy interjected, "He also needs tender love – like Mother asking JM to give her a little sugar."

The Senator said, "I haven't heard that since I was a kid. My grandmother was always saying, 'Come here and give me a little sugar.' Why do we adults refuse to remember the important things our grandparents have taught us?"

Jim shook his head and said, "Because when we're young adults, we think we know everything. It takes age and wisdom to realize we don't know the important things."

Catching him completely off guard she asked, "Sir, have you ever thought about running for Senator?"

Smiling, he answered, "No, ma'am, I haven't."

In a matter-of-fact voice she said, "Well, you should. We'll talk more about that later. Thanks for your candor. I found out what I wanted to know. What a waste of life."

After the Senator left, Jim pulled Mandy into his arms and whispered into her ear, "Wifey, I was wasting my life until you came along. When something like this happens, it makes you see what's truly important. Believe me; Sue has had more than her fair share of trouble. She was raped in front of her boys; then when her husband confronted the cop that did it, he was shot and killed. Of course, the cop justified what happened as being in the line of duty and everybody looked the other way. That left her with two boys to raise on her own. On top of that, her husband's parents didn't believe it was rape and to this day think she's just a slut and cut all ties with her and the boys. I think Sue was just looking for some kind of happiness; however, her luck ran out. Let's call Mother and Mike to come down and get Sue's boys. They're going to need all of the love and support they can get."